To my friend

Best wishes f...

Mountain Man friend,

Jerry "Old Jonah" Venicia

7/19/98   Thanks

And
Biskit

ISBN 1-891029-01-0

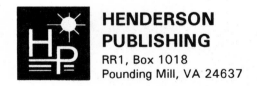

**HENDERSON
PUBLISHING**
RR1, Box 1018
Pounding Mill, VA 24637

OLD JONAH'S
BOOK OF
TALL TALES

By
Jerry W. Vencill

Designed and Illustrated
By
Ken W. Henderson

This hyar book is dedicated to my mother and the wonderful people who live in these hyar Clinch Mountains of Southwest Virginny. Many family names are mentioned in this Book of Tall Tales. Without the inspiration of the people and the atmosphere of the Appalachians, this book would not be possible. ---JWV

INTRODUCTION

Let me say from the start that I do not consider myself a writer. I am a storyteller; a teller of tales. So, I got to thinking, if I can tell them, I can put them on paper. And that's what I've done. Everyone likes a tall tale and believe me, they don't get much taller than the ones in this book.

I choose to write my books in the Appalachian Mountain dialect as a way of preserving it, as well as to pass it along to people who might enjoy it, but do not come in contact with the mountain dialect often.

We, here in the Appalachian Mountains, have often been ridiculed and labeled *hillbilly* and *ignorant* because of our speech and our ways. In truth, many people do not understand that our language is a true language, taken from the Old English language. And our ways have kept us going through years of hardships and trials. Up here in the mountains, we call it, *"good 'ol common sense."*

Today, in the mountains of Southwest Virginia, some people, myself included, still speak words and phrases from the Old English language. They speak such words as: hyar, thar, and over yander and phrases such as *"Ye best git hit fer me, I'm jist too tard to move airy a inch"* or *"Git hit out'n hyar afore I knock a knot on yer haid."* I have added a glossary of these mountain words to help you better understand the stories as you read them.

I hope you have as much fun reading them as I did writing them.

Jerry "Old Jonah" Vencill

Jerry "Old Jonah" Vencill grew up in during the 1950s and early 1960s in the Clinch Mountains of Southwest Virginia when storytelling was still an important part of life in the rural areas of Southwest Virginia. Many people still did not own TVs and shopping malls and video games were still a long way off. So, storytelling was still the best entertainment to be found. Old Jonah's dad was a true mountaineer with a story or a tall tale always ready. Whether it was driving to Little Tumbling Creek to catch a trout or Lick Creek to hunt squirrels, Old Jonah never found it hard to coax a story from his dad. It was at an early age that Jerry "Old Jonah" Vencill realized the importance of storytelling and that it must be kept alive for all those to come.

Having had it handed down to him by his dad, he has tried for several years to preserve the art of storytelling through a character he created called "Old Jonah, the Storyteller." Dressed in his buckskins, wearing a hat of racoon, skunk or fox skin, and carrying a long flintlock rifle, he travels all over the country, keeping alive the tradition of storytelling.

Old Jonah and his dog, Biskit still reside in the mountains of Southwest Virginia. You may catch a glimpse of him on the trout streams or at his favorite eating establishment at Claypool Hill.

Illustrator and Publisher Ken W. Henderson has been an illustrator for over forty years and now resides in the Paintlick section of the Clinch Mountains. His work in the stories of this book were drawn in pen and ink to reflect the illustrations as they might have been in the old days of printing.

Contents

Old Jonah and the Wonderful,
Magical, Talking Turkey 1

Uncle Jack 11

Tater 23

The Booger Thang 39

Me 'n Dan'l 69

The Big Wind 81

The Kantankerous Ginsang Root 91

The Aig 101

The Caves 111

Good 'n Urly 125

Glossary 133

Foreword

When I step out of the laurel bushes that border the thick trees of the Clinch Mountains, and I gaze down from the high cliffs overlooking Ward's Cove, part of the "stompin' grounds" of my Dad as a boy, I thank the Good Lord for letting me grow up in a time when people still cared for each other and they were willing to lend a helping hand.

Sadly, as I grow older, I don't see as much of this anymore. We live in such a hurry-hurry, rush-rush world, now, that there's no time to look deeper than the surface, although the good old days of the past aren't buried that deep.

Before me I see the dams of beaver, the eagle, and red-tailed hawk, and the little stream called Red Creek, flowing into the larger Big Tumbling Creek. Native trout dart into hiding as they see my shadow. I drink in all these wonderful sights and I am so very proud to be a part of God's wonderful world . . . . a part of the Clinch Mountains of Appalachia....JWV

Theys many a strange thang happens in the mountains 'uv Southwest Virginny. Yessiree! An this hyar little tale is 'bout one 'uv them strange thangs.

Old Jonah and the
Wonderful, Magical, Talking Turkey

Hit had been a long, hard 'n hungry winter. I'd 'et everthang they wuz in the house 'n I'se down to eatin' moccasin leather 'n chompin' on table laigs. I mean to tell you, my belly had done growed to my backbone. Why, you cudn't git a rye straw betwixt 'em.

The snow finally melted e'nuff so's I cud git the door open jist a crack 'n I seed I'se in a little truble. Hit'ud snowed so much, hit had snowed my cabin over. Only thang stickin' out wuz jist the tip 'uv my chimbly.

1

Wal, now, I thunk on hit fer a mite. I grabbed up my 'ol rifle gun 'n my powderhorn 'n sum lead. I tuk off my moccasins 'n got me sum toe holds 'n shinnied up the inside 'uv that chimbly 'n cum out on the cabin roof. I set down on the chimbly top, put my moccasins back on 'n whistled fer my 'ol dog, Biskit.

We started off fer the woods to see if'n I cudn't git us sum fresh meat. But, I didn't git fer 'cuz the snow wuz so deep. I had to go to the barn 'n dig out the door so's I cud git inside and git my snowshoes.

2

Atter I got my snow-shoes on, I started out agin. The goin' wuz a whole lot easier then.

I kept hearin' Biskit a-barkin', but I cudn't see him nowhurs. I looked fer a spell 'n jist when I'se 'bout ready to give up, I seed him way down at the bottom 'uv one 'uv my footprints. He'd done fell in afore I put on my snowshoes 'n he cudn't git out.

I had to go back to the barn 'n git my 'ol wooden ladder, climb down thar 'n git him out. I made him four snowshoes 'n put 'em on him. He wuz as tickled as a toad frog 'uv his new shoes 'n atter that, he got along jist fine. But, that wuz shore sum deep snow.

Atter 'bout four hours, we got out'uv the front yard an into the woods.

We travelled on an travel-led on 'til we cum to a waterfall. An hit wuz froze!

Yep, right thar in mid air wuz 'bout ten big 'ol trout,

3

standin' on thur tails. They'd jumped up out'uv the water an hit wuz so cold they froze right thar in mid air.

I opened my 'ol huntin' pouch, picked them trout right off'n the waterfall 'n drapped 'em in. I wuz gwine to have me a nice mess 'uv trout tonight, even if I didn't git nuthin' else.

Me 'n Biskit travelled on a little ways more 'til we cum to a little place thar in the woods whur they wudn't nary a bit 'uv snow fer 'bout fifty foot. Jist bare ground! Nary a bit 'uv snow!

I heerd a big whurrin' commotion over my head 'n I looked up. I seed twenty-seven woodpeckers with thur bills froze into the trees. They wuz a-flappin' 'n a-flutterin' thur wings so hard, they'd done blowed all the snow off and left jist bare ground.

Wal, all I knowed fer 'em to do wuz keep on a-flutterin' 'n a-floppin' 'til sprang, when the trees thawed 'n let loose 'uv thur bills.

I set down on a log thar in the clearin' 'n cut me off a chaw 'uv terbacker. I'se settin' thar a-chawin' 'n a-spittin' when 'ol Biskit opened up in that deep-throated growl 'uv his'n. He wuz a-growlin' at a big hole in a tree 'bout twenty foot away.

I got up 'n went over 'n had me a peek in that hole. Wal, slap me 'crost the noggin' with a pan 'uv corn pone, if'n thar didn't set a big 'ol turkey gobbler! Biggest'n I'd ever seed!

My 'ol belly started into rumblin' 'n a-growlin' like a thunder storm doin' flip flops, 'cuz I cud already smell him roastin' over a hot far in my cabin. I cocked my 'ol rifle gun, tuk me a bead on him 'n I started to pull the trigger.

Now, if'n I ain't a lop-yared mule, that 'ol turkey spoke right up 'n says, "Howdy, neighbor! Nice day, hain't it."

Dagnabit, I swallered that chaw 'uv terbaker 'n dang nigh choked to death.

Wal, sir, when I got thru chokin' 'n commenced to git my breath back, I looked at that 'ol gobbler 'n says, "Uh, wud....uh you mind sayin' that agin?"

He shuk his big, long beard, cocked his head to one side, 'n says, "I said, howdy, neighbor, nice day, hain't it. Whut brangs you way out hyar?"

I rared back on my heels 'n I said, "I'm a-lookin' fer sumthin' to eat. Hit's been a long time since I've 'et anythang but moccasin leather 'n I'm dang nigh starved to death!"

"Wal, that thar's too bad," says that 'ol turkey. "Wish't theys sumthin' I cud do to help."

"Oh, they is!" I says. "I'm agwine to shoot ye 'n take ye home fer dinner!"

That 'ol turkey jist blinked his eye at me 'n says, "Now, you don't want to shoot me. Why, they ain't that much 'uv me to eat. Now, on the other hand, if'n you don't shoot me, maybe I kin give you sumthin' that will suit you better."

"Wal, now, I reckon I got 'bout everthang I need," I says. "I got me a good rifle gun 'n a good hound dog. The onliest thang I hain't got is sumthin' to eat."

"Wal, pull my pully bone 'n dust my feathers!" said that 'ol gobbler, hoppin' out'uv that hole in the tree. "Why didn't you say so! Why, I'm a magic turkey 'n all I gotta do is flap my wings 'n I kin git you anythang you want to eat."

He flapped his wings onc't 'n out 'uv the air fell a red 'n white checkered table cloth, forks, spoons, plates 'n cups. Everthang you need to eat with.

He jumped up on a tree limb, flapped his wings agin 'n out'uv the air fell a big pot 'uv venison stew, a big roasted bar ham 'n a big pone 'uv steamin' hot cornbread, jist drippin' with fresh yaller butter. He rared back 'n flapped his wings agin 'n down fell a choklit cake, big as a worsh tub 'n a hot apple pie that'ud make yer mouth water.

Yessir, He give them wings one more flap 'n down cum a jug 'uv sweet apple cider 'n a big, foamin' pitcher 'uv cold, sweet milk.

Me 'n that turkey 'n 'ol Biskit set thar in that clearin'

'n 'et 'til we dang nigh busted.

Then, that 'ol turkey up'd 'n flapped his wings and tablecloth, forks, plates, 'n everthang else jist disappeared in thin air; all but whut wuz left 'uv the food an I hung into that.

I set thar on a stump a-pickin' my teeth 'n a-rubbin' my 'ol belly 'cuz hit wuz stretched tighter'n a banjer head. Lordy, I'd not 'et like that in a month 'uv Sundays.

I says to 'ol gobbler, I says, "Now, that thar wuz a mighty slick trick, makin' all that stuff disappear. That way, you won't have to worsh no dishes.

He laughed. He had a funny laugh. Hit sounded like, "Heh heh, gobble, gobble, heh!"

Wal, I thanked him 'n stuffed whut wuz left 'uv that bar meat 'n corn pone in my huntin' pouch fer later on 'n me an Biskit started fer home.

We got jist 'bout fifty yards frum my cabin when we heerd a noise. Hit wuz kind 'uv a scratchin' noise. I looked back 'n put me down fer a sore-yared polecat! Thar wuz that turkey a-ploddin' along behind us a-draggin' his wing tips on the snow. That's whut wuz makin' all the noise.

I says, "Whut in tarnation air ye a-doin' hyar?"

"Wal", he says, "I've done tuk a like'n to you an as long as I keep you fed, you don't need to eat me. So's I figgered we'd jist live together. Hit gits awful lonely out yander in the woods by yerself."

I invited him in an we all lived together an got along purty well, cum to thank 'uv hit. An I never had to go out lookin' fer food ever agin. We jist set thar 'n 'et, 'n 'et 'n got fatter 'n fatter 'n fatter 'til . . . Ka-blam, Wham!

9

Heh, heh, heh, ye thought we busted, didn't ye, heh? But what happened wuz the bench we wuz all settin' on broke. Heh, heh!

Oh, by the way, if'n you cum by to visit, jist lift the latch 'n cum on in. Theys plenty to eat 'n drank.

A Clinch Mountain man allus seemed to have a dog around him. He raised 'em an he hunted 'em an he loved 'em. He'd go thru far fer 'em an when one 'uv 'em died, he grieved fer hit jist like hit wuz family. 'Cuz, Mister, hit wuz.

Uncle Jack

Uncle Jack had allus been a hunter. I hain't shore if'n hits true 'er not, but I've heerd Pap tell that three days atter he wuz born, Uncle Jack crawled out 'uv his maw's

Uncle Jack

arms, kicked the cat out'n hit's skin, wropped hit around him, grabbed up his pappy's 'ol rifle gun, went out an shot a deer, skint hit out an told his maw to make him a pair 'uv deerskin britches, jist like his paw's.

Uncle Jack hunted all kinds 'uv critters, but bar huntin' wuz the kind'uv huntin' he liked best. He liked the noise the dogs made whilst they wuz chasin' the bar.

Sumtimes, on Saterd'y nights, he'd go over to Uncle Ras's. Him an Uncle Ras an Clarence an sum other 'ol boys wud take off an not cum draggin' in home til the middle 'uv the next week. They allus had a big 'ol black bar to split up amongst 'em.

11

Uncle Jack, Jasper 'n Leed

12

I don't know if'n you'uns ever 'et bar meat afore. Now, I shorely do love hit. I like hit a heap better'n deer meat. Hit's like real dark roast beef, only a whole lot more stringy. Hit's mighty rich, too. So's you kant eat too much at one settin' 'er hit'll give you a turible belly ache.

My aunt May, Uncle Ras's wife, uster to bile that bar meat with a onyun (that tuk a little 'uv the wild taste out'uv hit.) Then she salted an peppered hit 'n put hit in the old cook stove oven 'n baked hit. Put me down fer a lop-yared coon dog, if'n that wudn't the best stuff I've ever 'et in my whole born days.

'Course I never did know when to quit eatin' hit 'n I've had myself many a bellyache. An I've spent quite a bit 'uv time in that little 'ol house out back.

Wal, anyhow, they'd split up that 'ol bar betwixt 'em. One time one 'uv 'em wud git the bar hide an next time another'un wud git hit. So's atter a while, everbody got sum bar hides. They'd tan the hides an use 'em fer bed kivers 'er a rug fer the floor 'er fer whutever suited 'em.

Now, the reason I went into all that wuz to show you how much Uncle Jack loved to bar hunt. Yep, he loved to hunt 'em an he loved to eat 'em.

Uncle Jack had six 'er eight bar dogs. I mean to tell you, they wuz big and mean an jist flat out vagrus.

Uncle Jack loved all his dogs, but he had two, Jasper an Leed, that he loved better'n anythang. He'd been offered several thousand dollars fer 'em, but he flat turned 'em down ever time.

One day, Uncle Jack found sum 'uv his sheep missin' 'n atter lookin' most 'uv the mornin', he found whut wuz left 'uv 'em. He knowed hit had to be a big 'ol bar whut 'et 'em up. 'Cuz, right thar on the ground next to a few bones 'n sum wool, wuz big bar tracks.

Uncle Jack wuz mad e'nuf to spit splinters 'bout his sheep 'n he tried to git up a bunch to go atter the bar. But, everbody wuz busy doin' sumthin' else 'n he cudn't find nobody to go with him.

Wal, sir, that didn't stop him! Not fer a little bit. He'd hunted many times by hisself. Jist him an his dogs, 'n by thunder, he'd do hit agin.

Now, hit ain't a good idee to go traipsin' off bar huntin' by yerself, but many 'uv the hardened 'ol mountaineers never give a thought to hit. Uncle Jack grabbed up his rifle gun, let loose his two best dogs, Jasper 'n Leed 'n headed out to git that dad-blamed sheep killin' bar.

Uncle Jack follered them tracks up one ridge 'n down another. Mile atter mile he went. Mornin' passed into atternoon, atternoon into evenin', 'n evenin' into night. He wuz a long, long way frum home 'n now, dark had done ketched him.

'Course this wudn't nuthin' new to Uncle Jack. He'd spent many a night out under the stars fox 'n coon huntin'. So's all he done wuz build him up a far under a rock ledge, pull out sum biskits 'n hog sausage, 'n set right into eatin'.

Now, you kin bet the tops off'n yer brogan shoes that Uncle Jack saved a good part 'uv them biskits 'n hog sausage fer Jasper 'n Leed. 'Cuz to Uncle Jack, them wuz the best bar dogs ever wuz.

Atter they 'et, them two dogs curled up agin Uncle Jack an they slept nice 'n warm all night.

14

The next mornin' when hit got jist light e'nuf to see, Uncle Jack 'n the dogs wuz off on that bar's trail agin. By 'leven o'clock, they wuz so hot on that bar's heels, they cud smell him. (Jist in case you'uns don't know hit, a bar smells jist like soup beans that has been spoilt.)

Now, hit's mighty hard to git a mountainman lost. Dan'l Boone, when asked one time if'n he'd ever been lost, rubbed his chin 'n drawled, "Nope, don't know as how I've ever been lost. But I stayed bewildered one time fer three months."

But now, whur wuz I? Oh yeah, this hyar shore wuz one time that Uncle Jack wuz lost. He'd been so dead set on gittin' that sheep-killin' bar, he didn't watch whur he wuz goin' 'n got turned around worse'n a groundhog in a hurrycane.

Wal, afore he knowed hit, Uncle Jack wuz a-standin' in front 'uv a big high cliff 'n 'bout half way up wuz a cave. Not very big, jist 'bout the right size fer a bar 'er a man to crawl into.

Them two dogs didn't waste no time. They shot up the path leadin' to that cave a-barkin' fer all that wuz in 'em. The next thang Uncle Jack heerd wuz the snarlin' 'n growlin' 'uv two dogs 'n a mad Clinch Mountain black bar.

Afore Uncle Jack cud git started up the path to help his dogs, hyar cum that bar, a-waddlin' out to the front 'uv the cave. He wuz a-slingin' his big 'ol paws, a-growlin' an a-gruntin' up a storm.

Uncle Jack's mouth jist 'bout fell down to his knees. 'Cuz that thar wuz the biggest black bar he'd ever seed. He figgered hit'ud weigh clost to seven hunnert pounds. An

15

standin' on hit's hind legs, (which hit wuz), hit wuz ever bit 'uv six foot tall.

Now, Jasper 'n Leed knowed bars! Bars wuz all they'd ever hunted. They knowed how to rush in 'n dodge away frum the huge paws 'n sharp claws. They wuz a-givin' that bar one more fit. But thangs kin go wrong, sumtimes, 'n Jasper wuz jist a mite slow a-gittin' out'uv the way.

That 'ol bar jist scooped Jasper up in his big, ham-like paws 'n give a turible squeeze. Jasper let out a awful scream 'uv pain 'n went limp. (Uncle Jack said later, hit seemed like he heerd ever one 'uv 'ol Jasper's bones crack 'n splinter.) Then, that 'ol bar jist throwed him over the edge 'uv the cliff, jist like he wuz tossin' him back to Uncle Jack.

'Ol Leed tuk his eyes off'n that bar fer jist a second to watch his buddy, Jasper go over the cliff. That thar wuz 'ol Leed's undoin'. The bar whirled 'round 'n his long, razor-sharp claws ripped Leed wide open. Leed let out a whim-per 'n his life slipped away in a pool 'uv blood. The bar let out a roar 'n waddled back into the cave.

Uncle Jack seed both 'uv his best dogs kilt in a mat-ter 'uv seconds. He run to 'ol Jasper's side 'n cradled him in his arms. Then, he run to Leed 'n picked him up. But, both 'uv 'em wuz dead. Uncle Jack knelt thar awhile with his head bowed. Tears wuz runnin' down his cheeks like a river. Then he picked up Jasper 'n carried him to a big holler log 'n gently laid him in hit. Then, he went back 'n got Leed 'n laid him in the log beside Jasper. Uncle Jack piled rocks at each end 'uv the log to keep wild animals out 'til he cud git back to bury 'em.

16

Then, that 'ol bar jist throwed Jasper over the edge 'uv the cliff.

Uncle Jack struggled to his feet. Tears wuz streamin' down his face 'n he wuz shakin' like a leaf, 'cuz he wuz so mad over his dogs. He let out a roar, almost as loud as that 'ol bar, grabbed up his rifle 'n tuk up the path to that cave.

He walked into the cave, but he didn't go fer afore hit narrered down 'til he had to crawl. Uncle Jack wuz so tore up over his dogs, he never thought to be keerful. Afore he knowed hit, he'd done crawled right into that bar.

The bar roared 'n tried to grab Uncle Jack but he up'd with his rifle 'n pulled the trigger. The bullet went right thru the bar's neck. When the bar felt the pain 'n smelled his own blood, he went plum crazy. He charged Uncle Jack 'n one 'uv the bar's big paws knocked him clean out to the mouth 'uv the cave.

Uncle Jack picked hisself up, seed that bar chargin' him 'n his head cleared up in a hurry. He'd done drapped his gun, so he tuk off runnin' as hard as he cud. He said, sumtimes, hit felt like his heels teched the top 'uv his head.

He wuz miles frum home, but he shore wuz burnin' up the ground. He thought that 'ol bar wud give up atter a while. But, that bar wuz hurt 'n that bar wuz mad 'n he wuz gwine to make the one who hurt him pay.

Uncle Jack wuz a purty good runner, but atter several miles, he started slowin' down. That 'ol bar wuz gainin' on him. They run to the top 'uv the mountain that crosses over into Ward's Cove.

They wuz a family 'uv Mutters whut lived at the foot 'uv the mountain 'n Uncle Jack figgered if only he cud git to thur house, he'd be safe. He fairly flew over the top 'uv the

Uncle Jack wuz a purty good runner.

mountain. He went slippin' 'n slidin' 'n fallin' over trees 'n rocks, all the way down.

He plowed thru the creek so hard, he jist 'bout knocked hit dry. They wuz a rail fence 'bout forty yards frum the house. Uncle Jack started hollerin' soon as he cum to the creek. Hit wuz 'bout ten o'clock at night 'n everbody wuz in bed. So, he kept up the hollerin', hopin' they'd git to him afore the bar did.

The bar wuz so close, Uncle Jack cud feel his hot, stinkin' breath on his neck. An he cud feel the bar's slob-bers on his back.

Jist as he started over the rail fence, the bar caught him by the calf 'uv the laig. A turible pain shot thru his whole body an he felt the laig muscles tear. He felt like he wuz gwine to pass out.

Uncle Jack wuz in a real mess. The bar had one laig 'n Uncle Jack wuz a-straddle the fence with his other foot caught betwixt the rails. That thar wuz a bad sityeashun to be in fer shore.

His head cleared frum the pain fer a second 'n he thought 'uv his pocket knife. He managed to git hit out 'uv his pocket 'n opened up the big blade. He plunged hit into the top 'uv the bar's skull. The bar give a great jerk 'uv his head 'n the blade snapped off at the handle.

The bar give Uncle Jack a turific blow with hit's paw, knockin' him over the rail fence. The last thang Uncle Jack seed afore he passed out, wuz the huge form 'uv the bar fallin' on top 'uv him.

When he cum to, he heerd voices 'n felt hands tryin' to pull the bar off'n him. Mister 'n Missus Mutter 'n thur

20

young'uns had heerd him hollerin' 'n cum runnin'. They told Uncle Jack that Mr. Mutter had grabbed up his gun, but he didn't need to shoot. 'Cuz right atter the bar hit Uncle Jack the last time, hit fell over dead. He'd lost so much blood, he'd jist plum bled to death.

The bar give a great jerk 'uv his head an the blade snapped off.

They got Uncle Jack in the house whur Missus Mutter worshed 'n bandaged his cuts 'n bruises. She put sum salve on his laig, 'n bless my soul, if'n the salve wudn't made out 'uv bar grease 'n herbs.

Uncle Jack never did walk right agin. That bar had done tore out the whole calf 'uv his laig. Dr. Parsons, (he wuz a country doctor then, 'n the best around) patched up Uncle Jack's laig as best he cud. But that 'ol bar jist didn't leave much to work with. Uncle Jack walked with a bad limp 'til the day he died.

Atter he healed up a little, Uncle Jack rode his 'ol mule back to the cave, 'n with Uncle Ras 'n Fred Witt 'n sum more 'uv his friends, they got Jasper 'n Leed 'n brought 'em back 'n buried 'em on the hill behind the house.

Uncle Jack had that 'ol bar skint out. He tanned hit's hide 'n made him a lap robe. He tuk that bar skull with his knife blade broke off in hit 'n nailed hit on the front 'uv the smokehouse as a reminder 'uv that ill-fated bar hunt.

Now, this hyar hain't one 'uv them stories that you kin git a big laugh out 'uv. But, hit's true, fer the most part, an hit shows you how folks lived an whut they had to go thru afore all the new fangled ways 'uv today.

Back in the olden days, a "booger" wuz sumthin' used to skeer young'uns an make 'em behave themselves. Hit wuz a ugly, skeery critter, like Rawhead 'n Bloody Bones. If young'uns wuz bad an not mindin' thur maws 'n paws, they wuz told "You young'uns best settle yerselves down 'er a booger will git you." You never seed sich good young'uns atter that. Heh, heh, heh!

Tater

They wuz sumthin shore fer sartin at the bottom 'uv the river. Hit wuz as big as a worsh tub, round as a tree trunk an had a big, rusty rang in the top 'uv hit. An hit wuz stuck tight. . . tighter'n a porkypine in a thorny bush.

Hit wuz four foot under water an wuz jist plum puzzlin' to Tater. Oh, uh, Tater wuz Muley's cousin. You remember Muley frum Old Jonah's First Book of Tales don't ye? Heh, heh.

Wal, now, like I wuz a-sayin', this hyar thang wuz jist plum aggrivatin' to Tater. He'd tried ever way he cud thank 'uv to git whutever that thang wuz, out 'uv the river. He tuk his pappy's crowbar an pried 'n pried but hit wudn't budge. He dug a hole out beside the thang an got a big rock, laid a big locust pole on the rock, shoved hit in the hole an jumped up 'n down on the pole. Hit didn't move nary a inch.

He'd tried ever way he cud thank 'uv to git whutever
that thang wuz, out 'uv the river.

24

He hitched his pappy's team 'uv mules to the rang in the top 'uv the thang an yelled "Hiii! Git up mules!" The mules strained 'n grunted, pulled 'n tugged. They floundered 'round in the river 'til they dang nigh drowned. But, not one bit 'uv good did hit do.

Tater thought 'n thought. An then, he had a idee. He remembered the dynimite his pappy had stored in the smokehouse fer blastin' out tree stumps.

Now, Tater knowed he wudn't supposed to go near that dynimite. An if'n he did, he knowed his pappy wud tan his britches good. But, he jist had to know whut that thang wuz in the river.

One day, he ketched his pappy a-plowin' out the north field an he slipped the key frum under the milk can in front 'uv the dairy. He unlocked the smokehouse, slipped inside, opened the wooden box 'uv dynimite an tuk out three sticks.

Tater didn't know much 'bout dynimite, but he did know that his pappy put one stick under a stump. So's he figgered three orta blow out whutever that thang wuz, yander in the Clinch River.

Tater laid that thar dynimite down in the water beside that thang an lit the fuse. Ka-whoom! Boom! That dynimite went off an you never seed sich a sight.

You've heerd 'uv flyin' fish, wal, they shore 'nuff wuz flyin' fish that day! Fish went flyin' thru the air, into trees, into the barn loft, the chicken house an one even shot thru the half-moon 'uv the outhouse.

Tater's dog, Jumper, let out a squall you cud a-heerd plum over in Grundy. He started runnin' 'round in circles, chasin' his tail. He wuz 'causin' sich a fuss, Tater run to see

25

Ka-whoom! Boom! That dynimite went off
an you never seed sich a sight.

26

whut wuz wrong. Thar, clamped tight to Jumper's tail, with no intention 'uv lettin' go, wuz the biggest crawdad Tater had ever seed. Tater tried to pull hit off, but hit jist held on an pinched harder.

'Ol Jumper lit into howlin' louder an started jumpin' straight up in the air. He hit the ground an started scootin', tryin' to git that crawdad off'n his tail, an squallin' fer all that wuz in him. He wuz hoppin' 'n scootin' so hard, he ended up in the chicken yard.

'Ol Jumper lit into howlin' louder an started jumpin'
straight up in the air.

The big red rooster an the old gray goose seed that crawdad at the same time an they both made a dive fer hit. Each one got a-holt 'uv Jumper's tail in different places.

Now, pore 'ol Jumper wuz in a turible mess an a whole lot 'uv pain. He wuz runnin' 'round 'n 'round with a crawdad, a rooster, an a goose hangin' onto his tail.

Then, the goose grabbed a-holt 'uv one end 'uv the crawdad an the rooster grabbed a-holt 'uv tother end.

Then, the goose grabbed a-holt 'uv one end 'uv the crawdad an the rooster grabbed a-holt 'uv tother end. They pulled an they tugged. Jumper howled an that 'ol crawdad got longer 'n longer frum all that pullin' 'n tuggin'.

Finally, that 'ol goose socked his heels into the dirt, give a great big tug and that thar crawdad snapped smack dab into. Neither the goose 'ner the rooster wuz expectin' this hyar new turn 'uv events an hit caused quite a bit 'uv excitement.

The goose went flyin' backards. Splat! Right into the hog pen. The rooster went rollin' head over heels into the spranghouse, knockin' over the cream crock that had the fresh cream in hit that Tater's maw wuz fixin' to churn into butter, an spilt hit all over the ground. Jist rurnt hit all. You kin bet when Tater's maw found out about hit, she wuz gwine to be hoppin' mad. She had gone to the North field to take Tater's paw sum dinner 'er thangs wud 'uv been hotter'n they wuz already.

When 'ol Jumper found out that crawdad wuz off'n his tail, he lit out runnin' like a skeered haint. Straight under the floor 'uv the house, he went, and never cum out fer three days. I 'spect he wuz a-lickin' his wounds. Heh, heh.

I wud like to mention now, that the 'ol goose wuz havin' sum problems 'uv her own. Oh, she got to eat her half 'uv the crawdad. but not the normal way. An she didn't enjoy hit much, neither.

'Cuz, when she went flyin' backards, she landed, Kerwham! right on top 'uv the 'ol sow who wuz in the middle 'uv servin' dinner to her fourteen baby piggies. Hit knocked the wind out 'uv the 'ol sow an the goose, too. The goose got choked on her half 'uv the crawdad an, well. hit almost cooked her goose. Heh, heh, heh. Jist a little barnyard humor, thar.

When the goose landed on the sow, hit skeered them piggies so bad, they sucked in air instid 'uv milk, an all fourteen piggies got the hiccups. They wuz hoppin 'n pitchin' 'n fallin' 'n hiccuppin' all over the pig pen, jist like they wuz dog drunk.

The goose wud fly up an the sow wud pull her back.

This made the 'ol sow mad an as soon as she got her wind back, she bit down on the tail feathers 'uv that goose. The goose went to honkin' 'n floppin her wings, tryin' to git away.

But the sow had a firm grip. The goose wud fly up an the sow wud pull her back. Up 'n back! Up 'n back! Up 'n back! This went on fer a purty good while and finally when that 'ol goose got loose, she didn't have nary a feather left in her behind . . . nary a one! An I might add, she had considerable truble settin' down fer a few days.

Atter all the commotion died down, Tater knowed he didn't have much time to see if he cud git that thang out 'uv the river. His paw an maw wuz bound to 'uv heerd the explosion and wuz on thur way back frum the North field, runnin' hard as they cud.

Tater run to the river, waded out to the thang and give hit a tug. Hooray! Hit moved! Hit wuz loose! He pulled 'n tugged 'n now, hit wuz almost out! Jist as he made ready to give one final tug, his paw an maw cum runnin' over the hill. His paw started into hollerin' 'n yellin' 'n wavin' his arms, tryin' to git Tater to stop.

"Tater! Stop! Don't pull that out! You'll mess up everthang!" his paw hollered.

Tater heerd his paw hollerin' an he stopped pullin' an waded out to the river bank. Tater's pappy grabbed Tater by the arm and pulled him acrost his knee an wholloped the tar out'uv the seat 'uv his britches. He jist smoked 'em good!

Then he set Tater on a nail keg beside him, an started in to tellin' him a story.

"Tater! Stop! Don't pull that out!

"Many, many yars ago, yer great grandaddy cum into this hyar land frum over in Ireland. He settled down hyar along the Clinch River an built this hyar farm. He built the strong log cabin we live in now. He made a good livin', an raised a fine family. Everthang wuz gwine well and everbody wuz happy.

Then, one day, several yars atter he cum hyar, his cows started to disappearin', then, his sheep, an his hogs. He cudn't figger fer the life 'uv him whut wuz gwine on," Tater's pappy said.

"One night, they had done gone to bed, when they heerd sumbody run upon the porch. Whoever hit wuz, wuz screamin' an cryin' an poundin' on the door, beggin' to be let in.

Your great granddaddy grabbed his flintlock rifle an opened the door. A woman fell into the house. Hit wuz Annie Mae Jones! Her and her family lived 'bout four miles crost the ridge next to the Matt Marshall place. She wuz all tore up an scratched all over her arms 'n laigs frum the briars. Her clothes wuz almost tore off an she wuz bleedin'; frum a big cut on her head.

Annie Mae wuz only fourteen yars old but her hair wuz snow white! Sumthin had skeered her so bad that her hair had done turned white.

She wuz babblin' an a-saying' all kinds 'uv strange thangs. They got her in the house, give her sum hot sassyfras tea an calmed her down a little. But they cudn't make heads 'ner tails out'uv whut she wuz sayin'. She kept talkin' 'bout her maw 'n paw bein' dead an her little brother 'n sister bein' carried off by a big, ugly, skeery, Booger Thang!"

Sumthin' had skeered her so bad that her hair had done turned white.

Tater's paw went on. "They put Annie Mae to bed and jist as soon as hit got daylight, yer great grandaddy got his oldest boys an thur guns an they rode thur mules over to the Jones' place. They wudn't ready fer whut they seed when they got thar, though.

The cabin wuz plum knocked over, logs layin' everwhur. The barn wuz flat, too! Mister Jones and his wife wuz layin' in the yard, dead as doornails. They wuz crushed jist like sumthin' had stepped on 'em. The cows wuz dead. So wuz the hogs an chickens . . . jist layin' all over the place.

They buried everthang an went on back home. Poor Annie Mae never did git over the turible thang that happened. She lived on with yer great grandaddy an his family 'cuz she didn't have no more family. Nobody ever did know whur her little brother 'n sister wuz, 'ner whut actually happened at the Jones' place that night." said Tater's pappy.

He continued the story, "A few nights atter the turible tragedy, yer great grandaddy wuz ridin home frum checkin' on the few cows he had left. The moon wuz full an hit wuz as bright as day. Jist as he rode out'uv a clump 'uv trees, he seed a big thang whut looked like a man 'bout nine foot tall.

Hit's skin wuz all shinny like hit wuz wet an hit had a cow slungover hit's shoulder. The thang wuz headin' fer the river. Yer great grandaddy told how he follered that thang, makin' shore he didn't let hit know he wuz around. The thang went down to the river and went into a big hole on the river bank.

Jist as hit started into the hole, great Grandaddy said the thang turned an looked right at him. The moon showed

35

Hit's skin wuz all shinny like hit wuz wet an hit had
a cow slung over hit's shoulder.

36

full on hit's face. He said hit's face looked jist like a human skull an hit had a long tail jist like a big lizzard.

The next day, great grandaddy an all his boys (he had twelve) wuz down at the river. They cut down a big sycymore tree an made that plug you wuz tryin' to pull out. They drove hit in tighter'n a drum. Meant fer hit to never cum out agin ever. Then they dug 'n dug an re-routed the river over the hole."

Tater's paw continued, "So, now Son, you understand why you got that whippin'. You skeered the life out'uv me. An that dynimite cud'uv blowed you sky high. too!

If you had'uv pulled out that plug, hit's hard to tell whut wud'uv happened. If'n that booger thang really is down thar, we don't want to turn hit loose on this country 'agin." He put his arm 'round Tater's shoulder an they walked to the porch whur they worshed thur hands an set down to a big supper.

But, that night as Tater laid in his good, warm bed, he jist cudn't quit thankin' 'bout that hole in the river an the story his paw had told him 'bout the Booger Thang!

Old Jonah's
Rib Stickin' Vittles

In the olden times, when the injuns wuz still roamin' this hyar country, when a injun got a chance to eat, he allus eat 'til he made hisself sick. 'Cuz his way 'uv figgerin' wuz to eat all you kin, 'cuz you didn't know when you'd git yer next meal.

When I wuz a young'un, Maw really knowed how to cook. She'd pile hit out thar on the table 'n say, "Thar hit is, young'uns! These hyar vittles will shore 'nuff stick to yer ribs." These hyar tasty vittles will make ye set up 'n howl.

Taters 'n More

First, ye got to git ye a purty good size pot. Set hit on the stove 'n fill hit half full 'uv water. Throw in two ham hocks.

Cook 'em 'til thur almost done. Peel five 'er six big arsh (Irish) taters, cut 'em in half 'n throw 'em in the pot with the ham hocks. Peel five 'er six medium turnips, cut 'em in half 'n throw 'em in the pot, too. Throw in a pod 'uv hot pepper 'n slice up a red bell pepper fer color. Cook 'til the taters is tender, salt 'n pepper to taste. Drain off the broth (set aside to sop yer corn pone in). Put taters, ham hock, turnips 'n peppers into a bowl. Add a big dollop 'uv butter 'n git ye a big chunk 'uv corn pone 'n a glass 'uv cold buttermilk 'n ye'll be as happy as a hog in a feed trough!

*Sumtimes a feller jist can't leave well 'enuf alone. Most
'uv the time, hain't nuthin' you kin do 'bout hit. Ye got to
let him find out fer hisself. Jist like in this hyar little tale.*

The Booger Thang

Day atter day, as Tater went about his chores, he kept
thankin' 'bout that plugged-up hole in the river an the Booger
Thang that had caused so much death 'n destruction many
yars ago. Even now, atter all them yars, his paw wuz still
afeerd hit might cum back an start tearin' up the countryside
agin. Tater knowed that sumhow he had to find that Booger
Thang an destroy hit onc't 'n fer all. Only atter hit wuz
destroyed, cud folks live without fear.

One Saterd'y morning, Tater got his chance. His maw
'n paw wuz gwine into the settlement to git supplies an shop
a little. Any other time, Tater wud be rarin' to go along.
But, this time, he pretended to be sick; said he must'uv 'et
too many green apples the day before. An now, he had a
bellyache.

His maw made him take a big spoonful 'uv paragoric,
then they got into the wagon an tuk off fer the settlement.
Tater hadn't figgered on that dose 'uv paragoric. Hit wuz
bad 'enuf when you really had a bellyache. But, when you
didn't have one, hit wuz downright turible.

Wal sir, atter Tater got thru spittin' 'n worshin' his mouth out frum the bitter taste 'uv that paragoric, he set about gittin' his stuff together to go atter that Booger Thang. He tuk sum corn pone 'n souse meat, sum buttermilk 'n molassy cookies, a coil 'uv rope, his sling shot 'n coonskin cap. Tater tied all his stuff in a old tow sack an hung hit over his shoulder.

He waded out to that plug 'n begin to push 'n pull on hit. Hit wuz already loose frum the dynimitin' an hit didn't take much to git hit out.

Now, I don't know whut Tater expected to happen. Matter 'uv fact, I hain't shore he wuz thankin' a'tall. 'Cuz, when that plug cum out, hit sucked that whole river, Tater 'n all right smack down that thar hole!

I'm shore Tater wuz surprised when his feet went out frum under him an he went slidin' down, down, down that dark tunnel that didn't seem to have no end. Poor Tater wuz havin' a time 'uv hit! Hit wuz all he cud do to keep his head above the water. If'n that hole had been any wider, he wud'uv drowned. But hit wuz only three foot wide an so he wuz able to use his feet to brace hisself an push his head up fer air.

Atter whut seemed like hours, he seed way up ahead, a little bit 'uv light. Oh boy, he thought. Maybe I kin git out'uv hyar. An shore 'enuf, atter awhile, he cud see the end 'uv the tunnel. Afore he knowed hit, he went shootin' right out the side 'uv a mountain.

He landed in a little pond that formed at the foot 'uv the mountain. Tater clomb up on a rock in the middle 'uv the pond an wiped the water out 'uv his eyes. As soon as

Afore he knowed hit, he went shootin' right out
the side 'uv a mountain.

41

he ketched his breath, he begin to take notice 'uv whut wuz goin' on 'round him.

Not twenty foot away wuz a big toad frog in a black top hat 'n polka-dot bow tie. He wuz settin' on a lilly pad playin' "Little Brown Jug" on a fiddle, while a six foot black snake stood on the tip 'uv hit's tail 'n danced to the tune.

Tater looked over on the river bank an thar set a mammy catfish with one 'uv her baby catfishes bent over her knee. She had hit's scales pulled down an she wuz jist whalin' the tar out'n hit's backside with a fryin' pan, while hit's little brothers 'n sisters looked on. Seems he'd slipped an 'et all twelve 'uv his maw's worm pies that she'd baked fer the Catfish Social Club Jamboree.

Tater laughed out loud at the funny sight. The old catfish looked over at him an said, "Whut air you laughin' at, boy? You hesh yer mouth 'er I'll jist cum over thar an box yer jaws. That's jist whut I'll do if'n you fool with me!"

Tater seed a big green turtle swimmin' by, so he jumped on hit's back an rode over to the river bank. The turtle wanted to charge Tater a dollar fer the ride, but Tater said he didn't have no money. So, the turtle said, well, he had to have sumthin' fer the ride, so's he'd bite off Tater's big toes fer payment. Tater 'lowed how he needed his big toes, but maybe the turtle wud take a piece 'uv corn pone instid. That tickled the turtle an he swum off, a-chawin' happily on the hard corn pone.

He wanted to ask sumbody whur he wuz, but when he went towards the catfish, she run him off with the fryin'

42

pan. He went to ask the toad frog, but the toad launched into the tune 'uv "Froggy Went A Courtin'" an three more black snakes had done jined in the dance.

Tater heerd a stompin' noise behind him. He turned 'round an he seed a big black bull, standin' thar a-pawin' the ground. Hit's head wuz lowered an hit had the longest 'n sharpest horns Tater'd ever seed. He wuz bellerin' 'n bawlin' so loud, hit sounded like thunder when hit shuk the ground.

He grabbed his sack 'uv stuff an lit out'uv thar like the house wuz on far. He run fer whut seemed like five miles an ever time he stopped to ketch his breath, he felt the sharp tip'uv that bull's horns, pokin' him in the behind.

Then hit happened! Tater drapped his sack. When he stooped over to git hit, Blam! That bull hit him 'n knocked him fifty foot into the air. Tater flew right along up thar with the little birdies fer a while an then he started cumin' down. He landed on the top'uv a big round hay stack in the middle 'uv a big field.

He set thar fer a spell, 'til the buzzin' went out'uv his head an the stars stopped circlin' in front 'uv his eyes.

43

He seed that 'ol bull way back yander. Wudn't no bigger'n a flea. He figgered that dang bull done went an knocked him three 'er four miles, at least.

Tater slid down off'n the hay stack, crossed over the rail fence, an started walkin' down the road. He hadn't gone fer, when he seed a woman settin' on the fence, jist a-cryin' her eyeballs out. They wuz bouncin' 'round down thar on the ground, ye know. Her nose wuz seven foot long if'n hit wuz a inch.

Tater said, "Granny, how cum yer cryin' yer eyeballs out? Don't you know sumthin's lible to step on 'em an mash 'em flat."

The woman said, "Oh, sonny! I jist can't hep hit. I've drapped my needle an I can't find hit, 'cuz my nose is so long, evertime I try to git down on my knees to look, my nose gits in the way."

. . .when he seed a woman settin' on a fence, jist a-cryin her eyeballs out.

44

Tater got down on his knees 'n looked all 'round 'til he found her needle. He give hit to her an helped her ketch her eyes 'n git 'em back in her head. Atter that, she got to feelin' better.

Tater said, "Granny, why don't you wrap yer nose 'round yer neck 'n tie hit with this hyar piece 'uv strang I'll give ye? Then, you'll be able to git along better."

"Why, I jist never thought'uv that", she said. "I jist reckon I'll give hit a try."

She tied hit up an hit worked real good. She thanked Tater an he started on down the road.

He travelled on 'n travelled on 'til he cum to a little, bitty, log house. Hit cudn't a been but one room with a little old crooked stove pipe stuck out'uv the roof. An old man wuz settin' on the porch. He had his chur leaned back agin the wall, jist a-snorin' up a storm.

Tater walked up, rared back an said, "Howdy do, Uncle."

The old man said, "Howdy do, Son." An he pushed his hat back on his head.

When he done that, Tater jumped back ten foot, 'cuz he seed that man's face an he knowed that this had to be the ugliest man in the world. His yars wuz long like a rabbit, an wide as a elephant. His nose wuz big 'n round an the size 'uv a water melon an red like a mater. He had eye brows that arched upwards an wuz black as a crow. He wuz bald . . . didn't have nary a speck 'uv hair. His eyes wuz crossed an his teeth wuz bucked out in front an jist as sharp as nails. An to top hit off, he had a long black beard that reached plum to his feet.

45

Tater's mouth fell open an afore he cud ketch hisself, he blurted out, "Lordy, have mercy, mister, but blamed if'n you ain't the ugliest thang I've ever seed in my life!"

The old man let fly a stream'uv terbacky juice that landed right on top'uv Tater's foot, an he said, "Ye young squirt! Let me tell ye right now, you hain't no oil paintin', yerself."

Tater said, "I'm sorry, mister. I didn't mean no harm. I'se wonderin' if'n you cud tell me whur I cud find the Booger Thang?"

That old man let out a shriek, fell backards over the chur, rolled into the house, knocked over the pot-belly stove, jumped up, grabbed a side 'uv ba-con 'n a jug 'uv corn

46

squeezins an made a bee line fer the celler like his whiskers wuz on far. Onc't he got down in the celler, he stuck his head out'uv the celler door an shouted, "The Booger Thang! Oh, Lordy! Is he out prowlin' agin? Heaven save us all!" He grabbed the door 'n slammed hit shut.

Tater heerd him slide the bolt in place. He wuz left standin' thar all by hisself. He tried to explain thru the door that the Booger Thang wudn't nowhur 'round . . . that he wuz jist tryin' to find hit. But, the old man wudn't cum out ner say another word. So, Tater shoved his hands into his hip pockets an travelled on down the road.

Hit wuz gittin' purty clost onto late evenin' when Tater cum to a fork in the road. The right fork seemed to jist go on 'n on. But, the left fork sort'uv wound down towards the river.

Tater's paw had allus told him if'n he ever got lost, to foller runnin' water. So, Tater tuk the left fork. He walked 'til hit wuz 'bout dark an he cum to a little island out in the river. Right smack dab in the middle 'uv the island wuz a big buildin'. Hit looked like a church . . . even had a bell tower on top'uv hit. The building wuz all kivered over with vines an hangin' moss. Even the trees wuz hangin' with moss 'n vines. Everwhur 'round him wuz dark 'n gloomy an Tater thought hit shore wuz spooky.

The place smelled bad, too! Tater figgered hit must be stagnanted water since the place wuz like a big swamp.

Tater spied a little boat tied to one 'uv the big tree roots. He throwed his sack in hit, picked up a oar that wuz layin' in the bottom 'uv the boat an started rowin' towards the island.

47

The home of the Booger Thang.

48

Tater drug the boat upon the island an picked up his sack. He made his way up the vine-kivered path to the old buildin'. A big brass door knocker that looked like a human skull hung on the heavy oak door. Tater picked hit up 'n slammed hit agin the door three times. The sound echoed eerily thru out the gloomy swamp.

He started to slam the brass skull agin the door agin, but the door opened a crack an a wrinkled hand grabbed Tater's wrist! Thru the crack, Tater cud see an old man, all stooped over. He wore a black suit an looked jist like one'uv them butler fellers he had seed in picture books. The old man's hair wuz snow white an he wuz so wrinkled, he looked a hunnert yars old.

Holdin' onto Tater's wrist, he pulled Tater inside the dimly lit room. He said in a cracked 'n raspy voice, "Don't make no more noise. Ye'll wake him up."

An old woman dressed in servants clothes 'n lookin' a whole lot like the old man, stood in a corner wringin' her hands 'n moanin' over 'n over. "Mercy, mercy! Whut's gwine to happen to us, now? He'll be mad! Turible, turible mad! He don't like to be woke up too soon. Hit's hard to tell whut he'll do."

Tater said, "Whut's goin' on hyar? Who'll be mad?"

The old man said in his crackly old voice, "My boy, ye shud never, never have cum hyar. This hyar is a house 'uv pure evil . . . a house 'uv death. This hyar is the home 'uv the Booger Thang! An if'n he heerd yer knockin' an finds you hyar, yer life ain't worth a speck 'uv dust. Why have you cum hyar, boy?"

Tater told 'em whur he'd cum frum an told 'em the

49

story his paw had told him. He said he knowed that they wuz the brother 'n sister 'uv Annie Jones an that Annie wuz tuk keer'uv an treated good 'til she died.

The old man 'n woman both cried an said how happy they wuz 'bout Annie bein' tuk in 'n keered fer an how hard 'n lonesum 'n skeerd they had been all these long, long yars.

An then Tater told 'em. He says, "An now, I've cum down hyar to kill that 'ol Booger Thang an make everthang right agin."

The old man laughed a dry cracklin' laugh, "Heh, heh, heh. So, yer gwine to kill the Booger Thang, air ye? I jist wish that ye cud, son. I jist wish that ye cud. Cum hyar, boy. I want to show ye sumthin'."

50

He led Tater to a room under the stairs 'n opened the door. Tater seed a big room, piled frum floor to ceilin' with human bones.

The old man shut the door. "Thar, son," he said, "is all thats left 'uv the other brave young fools that cum hyar to kill him. Now, you better git out'uv hyar whilst ye kin."

Tater 'lowed, now, that wuz good advice, but he hadn't 'et in quite a while an he wuz tard frum travelin' so fur. An besides, he jist cudn't go back without tryin'.

. . . piled frum floor to ceilin' with human bones.

The old woman brought him sum food an while he wuz eatin', the old man told him more about their childhood . . . how hard they had worked an the turible thangs they had seed an had to do jist to stay alive. He told him how the Booger Thang had tuk their souls an put 'em in a glass box an how they cudn't die 'til he died. They told Tater that the Booger Thang kept the glass box in a big chest up thar in his room.

The more Tater listened to the old folks, the madder he got. He had got to likin' the old man 'n woman. The way they wuz treated jist didn't set well with him. He jumped up, slammed his fist agin the table an said, "Dagnabit! I'm so mad I cud eat splinters! Even if I end up like 'em bones in thar, I'm gwine to give that 'ol Booger Thang a tangle."

The old woman hugged Tater an said, "Yer a mighty brave boy, but I'm afeerd ye hain't got a chance. But if'n yer bound 'n determined to try, I'm gwine to tell ye sumthin' 'bout the Booger Thang that might help ye when ye tangle with him. I've told hit to all the others, but when they seed how turible the Booger Thang wuz, they jist drapped thur weapons 'n froze. Cudn't do nary a thang. An then he killed 'em 'n 'et 'em."

She said, "When I show ye whur he's at, don't ye dare let him look ye in the eye. If'n ye do, he'll hypnotize ye an yer a gonner, shore as the world. Now I ain't fer shore, but I thank I know whur he kin be hurt. They's a place jist above the tip 'uv his tail that's got a wide gold band 'round hit. An he won't let nobody git clost to that part 'uv him."

She led Tater up a windin' stair case.

53

Even if we git clost to hit, he bares his teeth an lashes them big claws out at us."

The old woman went on, "They's a place fer a key to fit into that gold band an he keeps the key in a pouch 'round his neck. Now, he gorges hisself an usually sleeps six months at a time. The six months is almost up an he's liable to wake up anytime. So, be real keerful an may the Good Lord watch over ye."

She clapped her hand over her mouth an looked up at the Booger Thang's room, real skeerd-like. She whispered, "That's the first time the Lord's name has ever been spoke in this house. If'n he heerd me, he'd tear me into little pieces with 'em claws."

The old woman turned a knob on the wall, beside the farplace, an a secret door opened. She led Tater up a winding staircase. Hit kept winding 'n winding plum up to the big bell tower. She slid a key in a big keyhole an Tater heerd hit click. She turned 'round an quiet as she cud, she run back down the stairs.

Tater eased open the door an peeked inside. Thar, all curled up in a big four-poster bed laid the Booger Thang!

Tater had only heerd whut he looked like frum his paw's story. He wudn't ready fer whut he seed. He wuz long 'n green an his hide wuz scaley. Long, matted an stringy hair hung frum the Booger Thang's head an fell down 'round his shoulders. His skull-like face had a horrible grin on hit.

The floor wuz kivered with bones. The whole room smelled 'uv rot an death. Tater's laigs turned to rubber. He felt the urge to run 'n hide, but then he thought, no, he'd

Thar, all curled up in a big four-poster bed laid the Booger Thang!

55

cum too fer to turn back. He had to make the best of hit!

Tater started creepin' acrost the floor, ever so slowly. They wuz ever kind 'uv bones everwhur; cow, horse, sheep an human jist layin' everwhur. Afore Tater's eyes cud git used to the dimness 'uv the room, he stepped on a cow bone an hit rolled acrost the floor. He heerd the bed creak an he froze in his tracks.

Atter a few heart-poundin' minutes, Tater started movin' slowly towards the bed. He wuz almost at the foot'uv the bed, when he seed the big wide gold band with the key hole He seed the pouch, hangin' 'round the Booger Thang's neck, too!

Slowly, Tater retched in his pocket an tuk out his old Barlow knife. He wuz glad now, that he allus kept hit sharp. He opened hit an quick as a cat, he cut the leather thong an slipped the pouch frum the Booger Thang's neck.

Tater breathed a little easier. "Thar, now," he thought. That much wuz done.

He tuk the key out'uv the pouch an placed hit in the key hole 'uv the gold band. With tremblin' fingers, he turned the key an eased the band frum off the Booger Thang's tail.

Thar whur the gold band had been, starin' Tater right in the face, wuz the exposed, beatin' heart 'uv the Booger Thang!

Tater wuz so surprised, he fell off'n the edge 'uv the bed, right in among all them bones, makin' 'enuf racket to wake up the dead. Tater made ready to run, but all wuz quiet.

He wiped the sweat off'n his fore'd. "Whew!" he thought, "That shore wuz a close call! I thank he's still

56

With tremblin' fingers, he turned the key an eased the band frum off the Booger Thang's tail.

asleep." Then his heart almost stopped. Fer a deep, slimey voice broke the stillness 'uv the room.

"So, my young friend, you cum hyar to destroy me, did you?" He laughed a deep, boomin' laugh that sounded like thunder rumblin' over a waterfall. "Well, I must say, you have cum closer than anyone else has ever cum. I admire yer skill an I'll savor yer flesh all the more fer it! Ha ha ha!"

An with that, he lunged off the bed, straight towards Tater, with his long, sharp teeth gleamin' in the moonlight. His sharp claws lashed out at Tater.

Tater backed toward the door, but the bones rolled under his feet an he went sprawlin' head first acrost the floor. The Booger Thang slammed his huge tail aginst the floor, tryin' to crush Tater's head. But, Tater rolled under the bed, jist in time.

Sumthin' sharp stuck in his side. He retch down 'n found a long, sharp sliver 'uv bone pokin' into him. He laid thar under the bed, holdin' that sliver 'uv bone an wonderin' whut in the world he wuz gwine to do. His side started hurtin' frum the sharp bone wound an when he retch down to rub hit, his hand touched his gravel shooter. He jerked hit out an then he had a idee.

The Booger Thang didn't know whur Tater wuz. He wuz screamin' 'n roarin' with rage, smashin' nearly everthang in the room.

The poor old people down stairs, wuz huddled together, jist a shakin' 'n prayin' fer all that wuz in 'em. 'Cuz they knowed when he got thru with Tater, he'd cum down thar an tear 'em to shreds.

Straight fer the open heart 'uv the Booger Thang it flew.

Tater laid thar under the bed, quiet as a mouse. The Booger Thang wuz gittin' madder 'n madder! All'uv a suddin, he grabbed that big old bed. Jist picked hit up like hit wuz a feather an slammed hit aginst the wall.

Tater tried to scramble out'uv the way, but the Thang's big lizard-like tail lashed out 'n hit Tater acrost the legs 'n knocked him flat on his back. The Booger Thang's sharp claws raked down acrost Tater's chest. Tater felt like far wuz searin' his whole body.

The Booger Thang moved in fer the kill! Tater, still in much pain, knowed if'n he didn't do sumthin' quick, hit wud be all over fer him. Quick as he cud, an bein' hurt as he wuz, he leaped on top'uv hit's chest, shoved the sharp sliver 'uv bone into the cup 'uv his sling shot. He pulled back an let 'er fly. Straight fer the open heart 'uv the Booger Thang hit flew. The sharp bone buried hitself deep, plum to the end in the soft beatin' heart.

The Booger Thang let out the most inhuman scream Tater had ever heerd. Why, the hair curled up on the back'uv his neck. The Booger Thang sobbed jist like a young'un. He begin thrashin' all over the floor, screamin' 'n moanin'. Atter whut seemed like ferever, he give a loud gasp 'n lay still. His heart had plum bled out.

The Booger Thang, atter long, long yars 'uv cruelty 'n terror, wuz dead!

Tater wuz out'uv breath, tore all to pieces, an plum skeerd out'n his skin. Never had he been in sich a mess. He wuz shakin' so hard, he cud hardly open the big chest.

But, atter he calmed down a little, he managed to lift the heavy lid. The chest wuz plum full'uv gold pieces 'n

jewels. An on top'uv all the treasure, wuz the glass box that held the souls 'uv the old man 'n woman.

Gently, Tater picked up the box an very, very keerfully, he carried hit downstairs. The old couple wuz still huddled in the corner. Tater set the box on the table 'n flopped down in a chur. He wuz plum tuckered out!

The old people run to Tater, full 'uv joy to see him alive, They brought him sum cold water an while he drunk hit, they kept him busy answerin' questions 'bout the battle. They jist cudn't believe sich a young boy cud do whut so many had tried 'n failed.

Tater rested awhile, then he went back up stairs. He tuk a ax 'n whacked off the Booger Thang's tail, jist above whur the gold band had been. He put the tail an the gold band in his sack. Tater tied a rope thru the handle 'uv the chest an drug hit downstairs. He told the old folks they cud have most'uv the treasure.

But, the old man said, "Son, we don't want ner need the treasure. 'Cuz we're a-fixin' to break that thar glass box an let our souls loose so's they kin git to heaven. We're tard. So tard. Hit's time we had a long rest." He cum down on that box with the poker frum the farplace an hit busted into a million pieces.

Tater felt sumthin' like feathers touch his face as two shadows slipped thru the air an out'uv the open winder. He looker over at the old folks an they wuz gone! All that wuz left wuz thur clothes and two little piles 'uv dust. They wuz so old, they jist crumbled away.

Tater tuk the chest 'uv treasure an the sack outside.
Then, he broke up a lot'uv furniture, poured sum coal oil
on hit 'n set hit on far. While the big house wuz burnin'
down, Tater put the treasure an his sack in the boat an rowed
back to the other side.

A crowd 'uv people started to gather when they seed
the smoke 'n far. Tater opened the sack an showed 'em the
Booger Thang's tail. The people cheered 'n cheered Tater.
They picked him up 'n carried him 'round on thur shoulders. They thanked him over 'n over agin fer settin' 'em
free frum thur fear 'n terror.

The people cheered 'n cheered Tater.

Tater tuk a sack 'n filled hit full'uv gold 'n jewels an put hit in his sack. Then, he give the rest 'uv hit to the people. He said goodby an started out to try an git back home. Everybody wuz so grateful fer whut Tater had done fer 'em. Why, even that mean 'ol black bull offered to give him a ride back to the hole in the mountain.

Tater tuk him up on his offer an had a nice comfortable ride on the bull's broad back. When he got back to the hole, he thanked the bull an then he set down on a stump to figger sum way to git back up that tunnel.

While he wuz settin' thar, the old mammy-catfish brought him a fresh-baked crawfish pie an thanked him fer settin' the countryside free. Tater wuz eatin' away when he felt sumthin' tuggin' at his britches leg.He looked down an thar wuz a big, long blacksnake. The blacksnake said in a hissin' voice, he says, "SSSSince ye went 'n ssset our country free 'uv the Booger Thang, I want to help ye ssss."

He stood up on the tip'uv his tail an give a loud, shrill whistle. Out'uv the bushes cum hunnerts 'n hunnerts 'uv blacksnakes. Each one tuk the tip'uv the others tail in hit's mouth, until they made a long, long, long rope.

The toad frog put on his top hat, picked up his fiddle an struck up the tune 'uv "The Blacksnake Boogy."

Slowly, the blacksnakes started crawlin' up into the tunnel. The big blacksnake told Tater to grab aholt 'uv his tail an they'd pull him up out'uv thar. Tater grabbed on an up, up, up they went,the snakes swayin' to the fiddle tune.

Afore he knowed hit, Tater's head popped out'uv the hole in the river bed. Tater thanked the snakes 'n waved 'til the last one had gone back down the hole.

64

The big blacksnake told Tater to grab aholt 'uv his tail an they'd pull
him up out'uv thar.

Hit wuz dark an very late an Tater's folks wuz still out lookin' fer him. When he seed thur lantern, he hollered to 'em. They cum runnin' hard as they cud.

Tater's maw grabbed him 'n hugged 'n kissed him. "Tater, whur have you been?" she cried.

Tater's paw, on the other hand, wuz mad as a hornet 'til Tater dumped that sack'uv gold 'n jewels out on the table, along with the tail 'uv the Booger Thang.

When his paw seed the tail, he went white as a sheet 'cuz he knowed whut Tater had done. His paw knowed 'cuz 'uv the story that he didn't know fer shore wuz true 'er not. A story whut 'caused his son to take sich a chance.

Tater's maw called him her brave little man. His paw wudn't shore whuther to thrash him 'er hug him. But he decided to hug him, 'cuz down deep inside, he wuz as proud as a possum puddin' 'uv whut he'd done.

Tater's paw helped him hang the Booger Thang's tail on the wall over his bed. Tater's maw 'n paw used the gold 'n jewels to make thur lives easier an his maw put sum aside fer his schoolin'. 'Cuz she said she wanted her brave boy to git lots'uv book larnin'. 'Cuz anybody that cud kill a Booger Thang, shud be president of the New Nited States.

She give Tater a cup 'uv warm milk, an rubbed sum possum grease 'n turpentine on his belly, whur the Booger Thang had clawed him. She tucked him into the warm feather bed, kissed him an blowed out the lamp.

Tater drifted off to sleep. He wuz happy, but he had night mares fer a long time to cum. Wudn't you?

BOOGER THANG
KILT BY TATER

Growin' up in the Clinch Mountains 'uv South-west Virginny, I've 'et my share 'uv Soup Beans 'n Corn Pone. An I've found they hain't nuthin' that sticks to yer ribs like soup beans 'n corn pone. But, now, I allus dockter'd mine up a little. This hyar reciet (many mountain people called a recipe a reciet) is one I thank you'll like.

Old Jonah's
Soup Beans, Corn Pone
(an all the fixins)

Soak a pound 'uv dried Pinto Beans over night. Next mornin', pour off the water an put the beans in a pot. Kiver with fresh water. Add salt 'n pepper. Throw in a chunk 'uv fatback 'er streaked bacon ('bout the size of yer fist). Cook beans slow 'til beans air tender. Cook more 'til the soup is kinder thick.

While the beans are simmerin' git ye a big bowl, crumble up sum corn pone in hit. Git a big onyun an cut hit up fine. Jist afore you pour in the beans, git a jar 'uv chowchow an put two big spoonfuls 'uv hit in the bowl. Then, pour in the beans, git a glass 'uv cold, sweet milk an dive in, like a duck atter a crawdad. Yum! Yum!

Theys been sum mighty important folks pass thru this hyar Southwest Virginny country. So, ye jist never know who ye'll meet out in these Clinch Mountains ner jist whut kind 'uv excitement ye'll find.

Me an Dan'l

Hit wuz jist 'bout dark. I'd jist finished feedin; my hound dogs 'n wuz settin' on my porch ketchin' me sum cool wind that wuz blowin' 'round the corner 'uv my cabin. Suddenly, the quiet 'uv the evenin' wuz shattered by the barkin' 'uv my hounds.

Then, a voice called out frum the edge 'uv the woods. "Halooo, the house!"

I eased my 'ol rifle gun acrost my lap an hollered back, "Show yerself, stranger! Keep yer hands whur I kin see 'em."

We'd had sum robbers waylayin' folks 'n breakin' in on isolated farms, so hit paid a feller to be keerful. Slowly, out'uv the woods cum a man. He wuz carryin' his rifle over his head to show he meant no harm.

"Howdy, stranger." I says, "Set yerself an rest a spell."

He sot down on the porch steps an I got him a cup'uv coffee 'n a plate'uv vittles. He shore wuz hongry an he lit into 'em fast. Atter he licked his plate 'n had a third cup'uv coffee, we talked a spell.

"Howdy, stranger." I says, "Set yerself an rest a spell."

He said his name wuz Daniel Boone, but said, I cud jist call him Dan'l. Said he'd been told to look me up an mebbe I cud help him. He said he needed to find a short route to the fort at Castles' Woods an he wudn't as familiar with this country as I wuz. So, if'n I wudn't too busy, cud I take him?

Wal, now, I'd heerd tell 'uv Dan'l Boone an hit tickled me that he wud cum to me fer help. But, I knowed they wuz tryin' to build forts purty clost together all up 'n down the Clinch River in case 'uv Injun trouble. An thar wuz bound to be Injun truble soon, since Old Hair Buyin' Hamilton up in Detroit wuz payin' Injuns fer white scalps.

Dan'l said his brother wuz gwine to be in charge 'uv the fort at Castles' Woods an he needed to find a short route so's Dan'l cud git him supplies 'n reinforcements when they needed 'em.

Hit wuz a funny thang to me. Hit wuz jist a few yars ago, the British wuz our friends, fightin' agin the French 'n Injuns. Now, they wuz our enemies. Seemed dang funny to me.

I told him that a feller by the name 'uv John Blackmore had built a fort 'bout twenty miles frum Castles' Woods an they didn't have too many folks to take keer 'uv hit. So if'n Injuns attacked, they wud be in a fix.

Dan'l spent the night an the next mornin' atter breakfust, we packed sum supplies an tuk off on a shortcut I knowed to Castles' Woods. On the way, we stopped at Fort Blackmore, whur we larn't that my friend, John Douglas frum over on Moccasin Gap, near Abingdon, had been kilt 'n scalped. That thar piece 'uv information left me feelin'

71

real blue. He had been a good friend.

We stayed overnight at the fort as the guest 'uv John Blackmore. Jist as we wuz gittin' ready to leave the next mornin', a man an his family drove thur wagon into the fort. You cud tell they had been in a big hurry, 'cuz 'uv the sweat on the horses. Them horses had been jist about run to death.

The man jumped down frum the wagon 'n shouted that a big party 'uv Shawnee Injuns had attacked thur cabin jist afore daylight. They had been lucky,though. They had the wagon hitched up 'n wuz cummin' to the fort anyway. So, when the Injuns attacked, they jumped in the wagon an tuk off fer the fort.

The woman wuz cryin'. She said when she looked out the back 'uv the wagon, she seed the Injuns settin' far to the cabin.

Even though we knowed the Injuns wuz raidin' all over the country, Dan'l thought we ort to try to make hit on to the fort at Castles' Woods. He wanted to warn his brother 'uv the danger.

We started out makin' good time. But, bein' more cautious than afore. In spite 'uv our caution, we run smack dab into a big war party 'uv hostile Shawnee Injuns an thur leader wuz none other than that low-down murderin' renegade they called Benge. He'd been doin' a heap 'uv killin' 'n scalpin' in these hyar parts fer quite a while.

Wal, like I said, we run smack dang nab into 'em. They set up a awful fuss, screamin' 'n hollerin' 'n then they tuk off runnin' atter us. Me 'n Dan'l turned 'round an made tracks back towards Fort Blackmore.

Hit wuz a race to see who wuz the fastest runner. But, Dan'l proved to be a mite faster. When we got to the edge 'uv the woods jist in sight 'uv the fort, Dan'l jumped over a log jist like a deer, but I didn't see hit an fell over hit, flat on my face.

Afore I knowed hit, two big painted Injuns grabbed me by my arms. Dan'l up'd with his 'ol rifle gun 'n picked off the one on the right. Now, hit wuz my turn. I grabbed the other Injun by the arm, twisted to the right 'n flipped him over my shoulder. He bounced off'n the ground an while he wuz gittin' up, I picked up my 'ol rifle gun 'n wholloped him acrost the head with the butt 'uv hit.

"I betchy he'll have a sore head when he wakes up!" I says to Dan'l.

By this time, the fort wuz awake an sum 'uv the men wuz fire'n' at the other Injuns frum off'n the fort wall. They opened the gate an me 'n Dan'l run in. They shet the gate back real quick. We kept up the fire'n frum the wall 'til we broke the Injun's charge. They faded back into the woods, takin' pot shots at us ever now 'n then.

They wudn't too many folks a livin' 'round them parts at that time. Most everbody had made hit to the fort. When the folks cum racin' into the fort in the wagon, an brought the news John Blackmore sent runners out to alert the outlyin' farms.

Me 'n Dan'l stood on the fort wall 'n discussed the sad sitiation the fort wuz in. Twarn't more'n twenty men, the rest wuz wimmin 'n younguns. They wudn't much powder 'n lead 'cuz the supply wagon hadn't got thru. An might not.

They started drankin' 'n dancin' thurselves into a frenzy.

I says to Dan'l, "On the other hand, they got plenty 'uv water 'n food. We'll jist have to stick around 'n help 'em when the gwine gits rough."

The Injuns slunk 'round jist out'uv rifle shot, showin' themselves frum time to time to shout sumthin' 'er taunt us in the fort. That kind'uv thang went on fer three, four days. I wuz gittin' mighty itchy, settin' 'round waitin', not knowin' whut wuz gwine on out thar. An I cud tell Dan'l wuz, too.

Finally, I says to Dan'l, "Why don't you 'n me slip out yander 'n see whut's happenin'?"

So, when dark cum, we eased over the back wall 'n headed fer the river. We cut us a holler reed apiece, slid under the water 'n floated downstream 'bout half a mile to whur the Injuns wuz camped. We crawled on our bellies 'til we wuz lookin' thru the bushes, straight into the Injun's camp. Whut we seed caused our blood to run cold!

They must'uv been three hunnert Injuns in that camp! An whilst we watched, two more groups 'uv twenty-five 'er thirty cum in. They started drankin' 'n dancin' thurselves into a frenzy. They wuz takin' turns paintin' each other fer war. They made a turible, vagrus bunch! Hit wuz enuf to make yer hair stand on end 'n dance Yankee Doodle!

Me 'n Dan'l backed up to the creek ';n made hit back to the fort. They throwed us a rope 'n we clomb back inside. We told John Blackmore whut we'd seed 'n he went plum white.

He said, "Lordy, we ain't provisioned fer that kind'uv attack! Maybe we better surrender."

Dan'l said, "Taint no use. They don't want no prisoners, jist scalps. That's Benge out thar! He'd murder us

75

all. No sir, we got to fight!"

When daylight cum, we braced ourselves fer whut we knowed wud cum. An cum, hit did! The woods wuz thick with Injuns. We cud see 'em gittin' ready. Then, with a blood-curdlin' shout, they wuz swarmin' up the hill towards us.

Now, thar wuz three good thangs these hyar folks had done. They had listened to John Blackmore 'n built the fort up on a hill, whur they cud command a clear view frum all sides. They had cut all the trees 'n bresh back frum the fort fer 'bout three hunnert foot. An they had dug a well in the center 'uv the fort.

Dan'l went one way, shoutin' orders 'n I went the other way. John Blackmore wuz in the powder house tryin' to see how much powder 'n lead he had on hand. They wuz 'bout forty people in the fort. We spread everbody that cud shoot, which wuz only 'bout twenty-eight, 'round the four walls 'uv the stockade. We wuz in a real fix!

The fort had one small cannon 'n we mounted hit on the front wall. We split the powder 'n lead betwixt the four groups on the wall 'n told 'em to make ever shot count.

The Injuns wuz 'bout fifty foot frum the fort walls when we let fly with the first cannon ball. Hit exploded 'n knocked five 'er six 'uv 'em sprawlin'. Dan'l give the signal fer his two groups to fire. More Injuns fell.

I give the signal 'n my two groups fired. More Injuns fell frum the deadly fire. Then, two 'uv our men fell frum the wall. The cannon fired agin 'n agin 'n then hit wuz quiet. We had run out'uv powder fer hit! Atter checkin' with everbody, we fount that each man had only two rounds

76

The Injuns wuz 'bout fifty foot frum the fort walls
when we let fly with the first cannon ball.

apiece fer thur rifles. We'd knocked down a lot'uv Injuns, but they wuz still a passel 'uv 'em out thar.

They wudn't nuthin' else to do but take 'em on hand-to-hand as they cum over the walls an hope they kilt us quick. Old Benge had been sendin' small groups agin us, but now he must'uv got tard 'uv playin' with us 'cuz he sent 'em all.

Ye never seed sich a blood thirsty horde cum tearin' out'uv them woods, screamin' 'n wavin' thur tommyhawks 'n scalpin' knives. Hit shore wuz a skeery sight!

A few 'uv 'em got to the wall 'n clomb over. We met 'em with rifle butts, pitchforks, 'n ax handles. I looked over on tother side'uv the fort 'n I seed Dan'l a-fightin' three at onct. So's I jumped off'n the wall 'n grabbed one 'uv 'em jist as he wuz a-fixin' to bury his tommyhawk in the top'uv Dan'l's head. I tuk keer 'uv that'un 'n give the next'un a good 'ol left hand uppercut, right under his chin. Sent him out like a light!

Dan'l finished the last'un 'n we seed sum more cummin' over the wall. Dan'l said, "Jonah, looks like this is hit! I'm sorry I got ye into this."

I says, "Wal, if'n hit wudn't hyar, hit'ud be summers else."

An Injun clomb over the wall, grabbed the bar holdin' the gate 'n swung the heavy door open. The Injuns cum swarmin' in! We formed a rang 'round the wimmen 'n young'uns 'n backed up agin the back wall.

Benge stopped his men 'n then he had 'em walk real slow, toward us. He wuz wantin' to see the fear in us. He wuz shore milkin' his victry fer all hit wuz worth.

An hit worked! The wimmen 'n young'uns who wud fight bravely to the bitter end on the walls, broke under the pressure. They started screamin' 'n 'cryin'.

Wal, now, I cudn't thank 'uv a worse fix I'd ever been in 'n jist as Benge started to turn his men loose, we heerd the flappin' 'uv wings overhead. A big bird flew over us 'n lit on top'uv the blockhouse. Hit looked like a big owl, 'bout five foot tall! Hit wuz as yaller as gold 'n hit had a glow 'round hit.

Them Injuns had a bunch 'uv plum helpless folks right thar afore 'em . . . a perfect massacre fer 'em. But, you know whut? Them Injuns throwed down thur weapons 'n tuk off a-hollerin' 'n squawlin'. Why, they wuz more skeerd than we'd been, if'n that wuz possible.

Even old Benge's eyes popped out 'n his mouth fell open. Me 'n Dan'l started towards him. We figgered to capture him 'n put a stop to his murderin' ways. But, he seed us 'n tuk off with the rest'uv his men.

We looked back up at that big bird 'n dust my britches, if'n hit wuz gone. But hit must'uv been a real bad omen to 'em Injuns to skeer 'em like that. All we knowed wuz hit saved our bacon, so to speak.

We jist accepted hit as another miracle frum the good Lord 'n thanked Him fer hit right thar on the spot.

Then we headed on to Castles' Woods. Just me 'n Dan'l.

Old Jonah's
Superstitions

When I wur jist a young feller, folks wuz a mite more superstitious than they air today. Maybe we jist tuk our time 'n paid more attention to the thangs 'round us. We larned frum 'em 'cuz sum'uv 'em superstitions had a lot'uv truth in 'em.

Take fer instance, when sumbody wud see a fallin' star, that thar wuz a sign that sumbody wud die that night. Hit wuz sumbody that lived clost to whur the star went down. I've knowed 'uv that happenin' many times when I wuz growin' up.

I allus did hyar tell that a haint won't cross runnin' water. So, if'n ye ever git a haint atter ye, ye best find a creek 'er river 'er sum kind 'uv water that's runnin' an not standin' still. In other words, a mud puddle won't do hit.

If'n a bird flys into the house, hit's a shore sign that sumbody clost will die. If'n an owl flies to a winder 'n hoots, sumbody will die soon. When an owl flies to your own winder three times in a row 'n hoots, then you will die soon.

These hyar Clinch Mountains have sheltered 'n perteckted her folks frum many a foul piece 'uv weather, blockin' out hurrycanes, tarnaders 'n cyclones. But, onc't in a while sumthin' real sneaky will slip in 'n git stuck. Can't git out! An then ye better watch out, 'cuz all thunderation will break loose.

The Big Wind

Hit wur the fall 'uv 1852. Everbody wuz hard at work, tryin' to git thur crops harvested afore early winter set in. All the signs wuz shapin' up fer jist that; a early 'n hard winter!

All the woolyworms wuz black as a crow all over 'n sum 'uv 'em wuz even carryin' little wool blankets on thur backs. Now, that's sumthin' ye don't see too much 'uv anymore. The bees built nests plum up in the tops 'uv oak trees, away frum the deep snow they felt shore wuz to cum. But, on the other hand, sum 'uv the bees buried dang nigh clear to Chiney, 'cuz they figgered hit wud be warmer way down thar.

The sheep growed 'bout four foot 'uv wool 'n they had truble gittin' thru the barn doors 'cuz the wool stuck out so fer. Ever night, the farmers got behind ever one 'uv the sheep 'n pushed 'n pushed, 'til they got 'em thru the doors.

Then, the next mornin', they had to go to the barn 'n push ever one 'uv the sheep back out. Hit wuz a whole lot'uv agrivation to the farmers, but they figgered by them havin' sich thick wool, hit must be gwine to be one heck 'uv a winter. An them thick coats 'uv wool wud cum in mighty handy fer the sheep.

The cows bunched 'emselves so clost together, ye cudn't git a wheat straw betwixt 'em. Sum 'uv the brown 'n black cows squeezed so tight together, they got thur milk mixed up 'n sum 'uv the white cows give choklit milk 'n sum 'uv the brown 'n black cows give white milk. Sum 'uv the cows that wuz in the middle got pushed 'round so bad, they give buttermilk, which made hit all seem udderly ridiklas. Heh, heh, heh!

The old cat wuz knittin' wool socks fer her kittens an the old coon dog wuz down at the still, runnin' off a batch 'uv corn squeezins to help him stay warm on the cold nights to cum.

Jist judgin' frum whut I've writ up to this point, I'd say hit wur gwine to be a hard winter.

Wal, like I said, everbody wuz gittin' in thur crops, a-makin' ready fer winter. I had already got everthang done. My barn wuz overflowin' with wheat 'n hay 'n corn. I had fifty-two pigs, forty calves, a hunnert 'n sixty hogs 'n I'd even marked all thur yars.*

I'd done cut up enuf wood fer ten yars. I kilt five hogs 'n had all the hams, tenderloins, middlin' meat 'n sausage hangin' in the smokehouse. I'd even picked five hunnert

*In the old days, people cut a markin' on thur hog's yars as a way 'uv tellin' 'em frum thur neighbor's. Hogs wuz 'lowed to roam free.

82

bushels 'uv apples, canned three hunnert cans 'uv peaches, pears 'n cherries, along with six hunnert cans 'uv corn, beans, maters 'n peas 'n I'd dug four hunnert bushels 'uv taters. Why, I even had twelve kegs 'uv home made grape wine 'n twenty fifty-five gallon barrels 'uv sweet apple cider 'n forty-eight jugs 'uv corn squeezins, all stored safely away in my celler. I thought, if'n winter didn't last too long, I had enuf 'uv everthang to git me thru the winter.

Thar I wuz, all rared back on the front porch a-smokin' my old clay pipe. My old hound dog, Biskit, wuz layin' stretched out by the woodbox a-nawin' on a grounhog bone. The birds wuz sangin' in the trees 'n thangs wuz finer than frog hair split seven ways.

Hit wuz 'bout one o'clock 'n I'd jist got thru eatin' my mid-day meal 'uv twelve yars 'uv corn, two fried chickens, a ham 'uv meat, three dozen biskits, 'n two grounhogs. I give the bones to Biskit; that's whut he wuz chawin' on.

I had a pan 'uv fried taters 'n I finished hit off with a apple pie, a blackberry cobbler, a pitcher 'uv sweet milk 'n a gallon 'uv coffee. I wuz feelin' right comfertible, although I wuz thankin' 'uv gwine back inside 'n finishin' off the rest 'uv that other apple pie.

The sun had been shinnin' bright when I set down 'n lit my pipe, but I seed sum shadders start to creep acrost the front 'uv the barn. The birds stopped sangin' 'n hit got as still 'n quiet as a grave.

I got up 'n stepped off'n the porch 'n looked 'round. Hit wuz shore a strange actin' time. I looked over at the chicken house 'n all the chickens wuz gwine to roost. The

83

He had his neck stretched out to crow, but nuthin' wuz cumin' out.

old rooster wuz standin' on the top 'uv the chicken house. He had his neck stretched out to crow, but nuthin' wuz cumin' out. Atter five 'er six tries, he give up 'n went on in the chicken house with the rest 'uv the chickens. A few minutes later, I seed him reach 'round 'n grab the door 'n pull hit to 'n lock hit.

I knowed sumthin' bad wuz gwine to happen . . . an soon! The sky wuz gittin' darker 'n darker an they wuz a yaller color mixed in with the blackness.

I run to the barn 'n locked hit down tight. Then, I done the same to all my out buildin's. I'd built down in a holler, clost to the Clinch River whur I had mountains on all four sides. I wuz in kind 'uv a little valley. Many's the time, I've seed wild storms go right over top'uv me, so's I wudn't too worried 'bout whutever this hyar wuz that wuz cumin'.

I started back to the house when I seed the slop bucket cum rollin' acrost the yard. Then, the wind started to pick up. I heerd a roarin' like I'd never heerd afore. Sounded like forty freight trains rollin' along amongst a buffalo stampede.

I run 'n locked up the house 'n jist barely had time to git down in my celler 'n shut the door. I set down on a bench to wait hit out. Even way down in the celler, I cud hyar the roarin'.

Then, I heerd a knock on the door 'n I eased hit open jist a crack. Thar stood the rooster 'n all my chickens 'n geese 'n turkeys 'n ducks. They marched right in. The rooster had a suitcase 'n the chickens, geese, 'n ducks all had thur nests an a basket full'uv aigs.

85

The rooster said, "Move over, we're movin' in! Hit's gittin' wild out thar! Why, the roof 'uv the chicken house jist blowed off 'n that seemed to be a good time to move in hyar."

Follerin' the ducks, wuz the cows. They had thur milk buckets on thur horns 'n the bulls 'n calves each had a bale 'uv hay on thur backs. Next, cum the hogs 'n pigs, pushin' a wheelbarrow full'uv yars 'uv corn. The horses cum next. They had thur oat bags hangin' frum thur necks. The sheep cum last 'n I had to go out 'n push 'em thru the door on account 'uv thur four-foot thick wool.

I looked around 'n the dog, cat, 'n kittens wuz already hyar; had been since hit started. I felt like old man Noah an his ark.

Wal, now, I'd be lyin' thru my mustache if'n I said hit wudn't jist a mite crowded. But, I figgered if'n hit didn't last long, we'd git by.

On thru the night the wind blowed. All thru the next day, 'n the next. Fer a whole week, hit blowed! I wuz gittin' a little edgy, listenin' to all the cluckin' 'n quackin', mooin' 'n neighin', meowin', howlin', crowin', honkin' gruntin' 'n baain'. Thar, I don't thank I left anybody out!

Hit wuz gittin' on into the middle 'uv the second week when I noticed sumthin' different. I went 'round 'n got all the animals quieted down. I had a little truble with two piggies. They wuz fightin' over a corn cob 'n you never heerd sich squealin' in yer life. I tuk the corn cob away frum 'em 'n one 'uv 'em bit me. I smacked him on his hams 'n that settled that! Both 'uv 'em went over to thur maw.

Wal, now, like I said, I cud tell sumthin' wuz different. Atter I got everthang quieted down, I cud tell whut hit wuz. The wind had stopped!

I opened the celler door 'n stepped out. I wuz afeerd to see whut had happened, but I shore wudn't ready fer whut I seed. They wudn't nuthin' familiar 'round me'; nuthin' I cud recognize exceptin' the farm. All my barns 'n outbuildin's wuz settin' thar, jist like they allus wuz, but we wudn't in Virginny. Dang blast it! We wudn't even in the New Nited States!

I'd seed kangeroos in pitcher books afore, but this hyar wudn't no pitcher book. They wuz all kinds'uv kangeroos jumpin' all over the place. All my animals wuz skeerd 'uv 'em. They wudn't cum out'uv the celler.

Then I seed sum little brown people! Them same pitcher books said they wuz pigmies. But they didn't look like pigs to me.

I went to my house 'n got my old school books 'n read 'n read 'til I figgered hit out. That thar big wind had done gwine 'n blowed me 'n my whole farm into Australia.

Wal sir, I give 'em little pigmy fellers a chaw 'uv terbacky 'n a keg 'uv my homemade grape wine 'n we set 'n talked fer two days. At the end 'uv the talk, I'd worked hit out with 'em to help me move my farm back to Virginny, down on the Clinch River.

The pygmies built sum big wagons 'n sleds. In jist 'bout two weeks, we had everthang back whur hit belonged. I told the pygmy chief (we had been good friends since I introduced him to our mountain refreshment 'uv corn squeezin's) that we ort to go down to the mighty 'ol Clinch 'n take us a good swim.

87

The pygmies built sum big wagons 'n sleds.

When we got down to the river, I shucked down to my longjohns 'n him to his loin cloth 'n we dived head-first into four-foot 'uv mud. That's right, mud! Don't you know that the mighty 'ol Clinch River wuz plum gone.

The pigmy chief went back to Australia, packin' four jugs 'uv my best hard cider.

An me? Wal, I moped 'round the house, feelin' sorta miserable 'bout my river. I mean, my chickens wuz back to layin' good 'n my cows wuz givin' milk good agin. Even the 'ol rooster wuz crowin' on a regular basis.

But, hit jist wudn't right without the 'ol Clinch River. I cudn't go swimmin'. I cudn't fish. I cudn't go froggin' ner nuthin'. Doggone hit! Whut bothered me most wuz I cudn't figger out whur the river had gone.

One day, 'bout a month later, I'se out sloppin' my hogs. I looked up 'n hyar cum Elmer Lee, the postmaster frum over in Cedar Bluff. He had his office in one end 'uv the old mill over thar, 'n he cum runnin' all the way over to my farm to deliver me a letter. Hit wuz postmarked: Arkansas!

He wuz as excited as I wuz 'cuz you know they wudn't much mail cum frum way out thar. I tore open the envelope 'n read hit. Tuk me a while 'cuz I only went to the fifth grade.

Anyhow, whut hit said in that letter wuz that they had our Clinch River out thar in Arkansas. Hit wuz in a big fight with the Arkansas River 'n hit wuz 'bout to whip the Arkansas River, kick hit out'uv the river bed 'n move in. They wish't I'd cum out 'n git hit 'cuz they had done got used to the Arkansas River 'n wud like to keep hit.

89

Wal sir, I got up a bunch 'uv fellers frum all over the Clinch Mountains 'n Clinch Valley 'n we went out to Arkansas 'n floated that 'ol Clinch River down the Mississippi, switched over into the New River 'n finally got her back to whur she belonged.

They wuz real happy over thar in Cedar Bluff, 'cuz the mill had to shut down 'cuz 'uv no water. An I guess hit's safe to say, everbody wuz glad to see that 'ol river back 'n flowin' agin.

Now, I knowed that this sorta thang cud happen agin. So's I set out to make shore we didn't lose the river, no matter how hard that wind blowed.

I got me several big thick cables 'n stretched 'em plum acrost the river. I drove locust fence posts four miles deep into the ground 'n tied them cables to 'em with double whammy knots. I put them cables 'bout ever ten miles, all up 'n down the river.

I wiped the sweat off'n my face 'n said, "Now, by crackys! Let 'er blow!"

Old Jonah
and the
Kantankerous
Ginsang Root

Ginsang, 'er jist plain "sang" to the folks whut live in the Clinch Mountains, has allus meant extry money. When the first settlers cum into these hyar mountains, they cum lookin' fer furs 'n ginsang. 'Ol Absalom Looney, the feller that Abbs Valley wuz named atter, cum hyar frum Augusta County, Virginny, lookin' fer them two very thangs . . . sang 'n furs. Now, they's all kinds 'uv sang. They's two-leafs 'n three-leafs. They're too little to fool with. Then, they's two-prongs, three-prongs 'n four-prongs 'n so on. Most 'uv the time, the more prongs, the bigger the root, 'n the bigger the root, the better the Chinese liked hit 'n they paid more fer hit. We sold a awful lot over in Chiney. Hit's got bright red berries on hit when hit is ready to dig. My maw allus said, "'Til ye larn hit, hit looks like everthang else in the mountains. But, onc't ye've larned hit, tain't nuthin' else in the mountains looks like hit." Don't rekon nobody ever found one as big as the one I found in this hyar tale.

When I first cum hyar to these mountains 'uv Southwest Virginny, I wudn't more'n seventeen yars old. I wuz like most 'uv the others that cum hyar. I'se lookin' fer furs, ginsang, 'n I'se also lookin' fer the right place to settle down.

Wal, I'm hyar to tell ye, folks, I found hit all; fur-bearing critters as thick as bees on a honeycomb, 'n ginsang growin' as high as yer waist, jist about everwhur you walked. An, to top hit off, I found me the perfeck piece 'uv land. Flat land, rollin' land, mountain 'n forest land, all nestled real snug beside the Clinch River.

What a time hit wuz, when I traipsed into that unexplored territory. The river wuz teemin' with ever kind 'uv fish you cud thank 'uv: bass, trout, catfish, 'n red eyes. You name hit 'n they wuz thar! The woods wuz full 'uv deer, bear, turkey, pheasant, quail, grouse, rabbit, squirrel, wild boar, 'n buffalo.

They wuz sum purty mean critters, too! Wolves, panthers, 'n sum mean, two-legged critters . . . Injuns. I'm hyar to tell ye, hit wuz sum kind 'uv country!

By the time I got a cabin built, crops planted 'n harvested, hit wuz late fall.

One bright, cool mornin', I woke up 'n while I wuz eatin' breakfust, I decided to go ginsangin'. I throwed me sum food in a sack, grabbed sum diggin' tools 'n tied hit all on the back 'uv my old mule. I picked up my rifle gun, clomb on the mule's back 'n headed out.

I rode fer a spell. I wudn't in no hurry. Hit wuz Friday 'n I'd done planned to camp out all weekend.

Hit wuz a little afore noon when I topped out on a mountain, overlookin' whut is now Saltville. I crossed a little creek 'n follered hit down into a deep holler. When I got to the bottom, I slid off'n the mule, watered him, 'n let him eat the lush grass along the creek bank.

While he wuz eatin', I walked 'round the clearin', jist lookin 'round. This hyar wuz strange, unfamiliar country. I hadn't never been hyar afore.

I tripped over a stick 'n afore I cud ketch myself, I rolled down a little rise into a gully. I retch out 'n grabbed a little tree trunk to pull myself up. The tree wuz funny lookin' 'n the more I looked at hit, the more hit didn't look like a tree.

Hit wuz 'bout eight-foot tall. I cud barely see the top, but, the more I stared at the top, the more hit looked like a ginsang plant. Hit even had a big pod 'uv red berries the size 'uv my fist.

Now, they's sum strange thangs hyar in these mountains, but an eight-foot-tall ginsang plant is a might uncommon. I says to myself, "Lawk a mercy! If'n the plant's that big, how big ye rekon the root is?"

I walked 'round the plant several times, tryin' to figger out the best way to git that ginsang root out'uv the ground. I throwed my arms 'round the plant 'n pulled with all my mite. But, hit wudn't budge! I tuk my sang hoe 'n dug out frum 'round hit 'til I found the top 'uv the root. I kept diggin' on down 'n purty soon, I had me a big, deep hole 'n a big pile 'uv dirt.

I tied a rope 'round the plant 'n tied the rope to the mule. Then I led the mule up the holler, 'bout half a mile. The old mule tugged 'n puffed 'n pulled. I seed that 'ol sang root slowly cummin' up out'n the ground. One foot, two

I threw my arms 'round the plant 'n pulled with all my mite.

foot, three foot! I tied the rope 'round a big tree, so's I cud git a new holt, but when I let out a little slack, the ginsang root shot back down in the ground. I hitched the mule back up 'n made another pull. This time hit cum out'uv the ground six foot. I got ready to make another pull, but as soon as a little slack cum in the rope, the root shot back down agin.

I set down on a stump 'n scratched my head. Sumthin' wuz definitely wrong, hyar. That dadblamed ginsang root wuz supposed to stay out 'uv the ground, not jump up 'n down like a toad frog. Sumthin' wuz pullin' hit back down 'n dadblast hit. I wuz gwine to find out whut hit wuz.

Lookin' 'round, I seed a big log 'bout twenty-foot around. Hit wuz solid 'n hadn't been down but a couple 'uv yars. I found me a stout hickery limb, big 'n round as my arm 'n I rigged me up a winder-upper do-fatchet, complete with crank. Onc't I had hit all tied up to that big log, I set down 'n started windin' up that rope.

Purty soon, that 'ol sang root started easin' up agin. Up, up, up hit cum. Already, ten-foot long, that thar wuz sum ginsang root, 'n hit wuz still cummin' up out'uv the hole.

By this time, my arms wuz shore gittin' tard. The root wuz six miles long, so's I figgered hit wudn't gwine to stop fer a long time. I rigged that mule to the crank 'n as he walked 'round 'n 'round, more 'n more root cum up. We worked all day Friday 'n all day Saterd'y on that ginsang root. I had to take my ax 'n chop that root into blocks 'n stack hit like farwood, elsewise, hit wud'uv reached clear over to Marion. (Sum say that's whur I ort to be, anyhow.) Heh, heh, heh.

I rigged me up a winder-upper do-fatchet, complete with crank.

When Sunday rolled 'round, I had 143 tons 'uv ginsang root, cut 'n stacked. I tuk the mule loose frum the winder-upper rig 'n hitched him straight to the sang root. Then, I lit a half stick 'uv dynimite 'n tied hit to the mule's tail.

Hit went off 'n skeerd the mule so bad, he jumped thurty foot in the air. That jerk wuz all hit tuk to brang that sang root out'uv the ground. Hit popped out'uv thar like a cork in a cider jug.

When that sang root popped out, I seed how cum hit had been so hard to git out. Hangin' on the very tip 'uv that root, wuz a old Chinese man with a long white pointy beard 'n a little pointy hat. Hangin' onto him, wuz a young man, a woman, an three young'uns, all Chinese. They jist kept cumin' up out 'uv that hole. Purty soon, I had about a hunnert people, standin' 'round.

They'd brung food, so's we jist set down 'n 'et 'n talked fer a spell. I cudn't talk Chinese, but the old man cud talk my language. Seems like they had been tryin' to pull the root out down thar in Chiney 'n I wuz tryin' to pull hit out up hyar in Virginny. We wuz pullin' agin each other. Then, I made my winder-upper do-fatchet. They didn't have one, so I got the sang root.

We finished choppin' hit up 'n then I give 'em all a armload 'uv ginsang 'n helped 'em back down the hole. I filled the hole 'n then I buried that big pod 'uv red berries so's they wud be more 'uv them big roots in a few yars.

I made five hunnert wagon trips back 'n forth to git all that cut-up ginsang 'n I had to cut a wagon trail all the way to git hit. By the time I got all that ginsang stored 'n

Hangin' on the very tip 'uv that root, wuz a old Chinese man with a
long white pointy beard 'n a little pointy hat.

98

dryin', the snow wuz startin' to fly.

When sprang cum, I tuk all that good, dried ginsang over into Washington County, over thar to Abingdon 'n turned hit into twenty-dollar gold pieces. I wuz glad I had my old wagon 'cuz I shore needed hit to haul all that gold back home.

Now, they's sumthin' ye ort to know. I didn't tell ye the whole truth about them red berries. The truth is, I kept a few 'uv 'em 'n planted them about ten foot frum the house. That way, I don't have to travel so fer to git hit. 'Til hit gits ready to dig, I can use the plants fer shade trees.

I jist hope yer next ginsangin' trip turns out to be as prosperus as mine. Yes sir, I jist hope hit does. Heh, heh, heh.

Old Jonah says . . .

If'n ye got a itch, scratch hit! An if'n ye don't got a itch, scratch hit anyway. 'Cuz one'll cum along sooner 'er later.

Count yerself lucky that the Good Lord seed fit to put yer head whur hit's at.

Sumtimes, hit's best to leave thangs that don't be-long to you jist whur they are.

The Aig

The rain wuz pourin' down in buckets when I seed the cave. Hit wuz jist a small slash 'crost the front 'uv a high cliff. I never wud'uv seed hit if'n I wudn't standin' in jist the right place when the lightnin' flashed, 'n lit everthang up, jist like broad daylight.

I'd been out tryin' to git me sum fresh meat 'n I'd hunted a little too fer frum home. Dark had ketched me 'n now I needed a place to git out'uv this hyar downpour.

I jist made hit to the mouth 'uv the cave, when a lightnin' bolt hit a big pine tree right above the entrance. Hit split hit in a hunnert pieces 'n sum 'uv the pieces wuz still burnin'. So's I grabbed me up two 'uv the burnin' limbs 'n carried 'em into the cave. Them pieces 'uv pine made dandy torches.

Onc't I had a chance to wipe the rain out'uv my eyes, I set about to build me a far. The rain wuz cold 'n I wuz shiverin' purty hard. My luck wuz runnin' good fer a change. They wuz a good sized pile 'uv sticks 'n dry grass in a cor-ner that a pack rat 'er sum other critter had drug in fer a nest.

I put hit all together, tuk out my flint 'n steel, struck me sum sparks down on that dry grass 'n afore ye knowed hit, I had me a nice little, warm far.

101

I fount me a couple 'uv holes in the cave walls 'n stuck the pine torches in 'em. The light 'uv the torches lit that 'ol cave up purty bright. Ye cud say that with the far 'n the torchlight, hit wuz almost cheery.

The rain kept cumin' down harder 'n harder. Twarn't a fit night out fer man 'ner beast 'n I wuz mighty happy to 'uv fount the cave. I dug me out a comfortable hole fer my shoulders 'n leaned back agin the wall. Afore I knowed hit, I'd done dozed off.

I dug me out a comfortable hole fer my shoulders
'n leaned back agin the wall.

I 'spect hit wuz 'bout one o'clock in the mornin' when I cum wide awake. Sumthin', I don't know whut, woke me up. I listened hard! Thar, hit wuz agin! I figgered hit wuz bats.

My far had died down, so's I tuk one 'uv the torches 'n looked 'round the cave fer sum more wood. Hit wuz my way 'uv thankin' that the cave wuz jist one little room. But, while I wuz lookin' fer wood, I fount I wuz wrong. Yessir, they wuz a low passage gwine summers further back into the cave.

I had to crawl thru the tunnel. Hit seemed to go on 'n on. I kept at hit 'n then, way up ahead, I seed a red light. Afore I cud say, "Scat, Yaller! Git ye tail out'uv the gravy bowl", I'd done crawled into a big room.

The red light turned out to be a red glow. I cudn't tell whur hit wuz cumin' frum, but hit made everthang red. I tell ye, the hair stood up on the back 'uv my neck. Hit wuz so quiet in that cavern, ye cud hyar a pin drap. The eerie red glow made me feel like I ort to git out'uv thar fast.

I started to back out'uv the tunnel, when I heerd that noise agin. Hit sounded like flappin' wings. Hit wuz cumin' frum the roof 'uv the cave. I held my torch up closer to the roof 'n thar in the torchlight, I seed a big hole right in the top'uv the cave. Hit wuz 'bout six foot wide 'n went straight up, like a smoke hole in a injun wikiup.

My foot slipped on a rock 'n I rolled down onto the floor 'uv the cave. When I stood up, I seed a big nest, settin' on a tall, flat rock right in the center 'uv the room. I eased over 'n stuck my head over the edge 'uv the nest. I 'bout drapped my teeth! Shivers run up 'n down my back.

103

I eased over 'n stuck my head over the edge 'uv the nest.

104

Now, I ain't one to be afeerd 'uv much, but whut I seed in that thar nest made me wish I wuz summers else. They wuz a big aig layin' in that nest. Oh, but hit wudn't jist no ordinary aig!

No siree, bobtail! Hit wus the biggest aig I'd ever seed! Bigger'n them ostrich aigs I'd seed in pitcher books. An, hit wuz red. That wuz the purtiest aig I'd ever seed in my life. All red 'n shinny. That's whur the red glow wuz cumin' frum. Frum that aig!

I retched out my hand to tech hit. Dang nab it! Hit wuz hotter'n a chigger on a far coal. Out'uv the corner 'uv my eye, I seed sumthin' move, over agin the cave wall. I looked down on the floor. Lawk a mercy! They wuz snakes! Hunnerts 'uv snakes! Ever kind'uv snake ye cud thank 'uv. Rattleheads 'n copperbellies! Hit wuz like they wuz guardin' that aig. I had to do sumthin' fast, afore they got to me!

So's I tuk my powder horn 'n poured a line 'uv powder betwixt me 'n them snakes. Jist as they got thur 'ol bellies on that line 'uv powder, I hit my flint agin the steel 'n the sparks hit the powder.

Swoosh! The powder went off. You never heerd sich hissin' 'n rattlin' in yer whole born days. Them 'ol snakes burnt thur bellies 'n they turned right around 'n crawled back whur they cum frum, whurever that wuz.

Wal, I figgered I'd been hyar in this place long enuf. They wuz deer bones, bar bones, even cow 'n horse bones, layin' all over the place. I got to thankin' that they'd probably be sum Old Jonah bones layin' 'round hyar afore too long. So's I picked up my torch 'n started back to the tunnel.

A deer carcass suddenly cum fallin' thru the hole in the roof 'n bounced on the floor. Hit wuz follered by a loud beatin' 'uv wings. I ducked back into the tunnel 'cuz I wudn't real shore I wanted to see whut wuz cumin' down thru that hole in the roof.

But, ye know how hit is. Ye don't want to know 'n yit, ye jist got to know. So I stayed. Out'uv sight. But, I stayed. Peekin' 'round the edge 'uv the tunnel, I seed a fearsum sight!

A female eagle, 'bout twelve foot tall 'n glowin' red, jist like the room, slid down thru the hole in the roof. Hit landed on the cave floor. She beat her wings 'n let out a awful scream! Skrawk!

I had to put my hands over my yars to keep my yardrums frum bustin'. She kept on screamin' 'til another eagle, must'uv been the male, cum slidin' down the hole 'n landed beside her. He set into screamin', too!

They must'uv smelled me, whur I teched the aig. I don't have to tell ye, they wuz mad. They lit in on that deer, 'n when they got thru, they wudn't a scrap 'uv meat left on hit's bones.

Atter they 'et, they started lookin' fer me! I scrooched up under a rock 'n lucky fer me, the tunnel wuz too narrer fer 'em to git into. But, when he stuck his big head up to the tunnel 'n seed me, he started clawin' 'n tearin' with his sharp, cruel claws 'n beak, jist makin' 'em rocks fly!

Hit wuz then, I noticed his eyes wuz blood red 'n his head looked sort'uv like a mountain lion's head with a beak. 'Bout the time he wuz gittin' close to me, the female eagle let out a scream. Hit wuz almost human.

106

. . .when he stuck his big head up to the tunnel 'n seed me,
he started clawin. . .

The male eagle turned 'n I cud see the aig. Hit wuz hatchin'! Lordy, hit wuz ugly! Hit wuz blood red all over an instid 'uv feathers, hit wuz kivered with a stiff, red hair. Even jist hatched, hit wuz six foot tall an hit wuz mighty hungry.

Now, I wuz in truble! 'Cuz he cud git thru the hole in the tunnel whur I wuz. An he seed me! He waddled over, stuck his ugly 'ol head back under the rock whur I wuz 'n bit my laig. I kicked him right in his Adam's apple.

He skrawked 'n stuck his head back in. I had me a chaw 'uv terbacky 'n I wallered hit 'round 'n got me sum terbacky juice worked up. I let fly a big squirt, right betwixt his 'ol crossed eyes.

That done it! He fell backards 'n started rollin' 'n floppin' like a chicken whut done had hit's neck rung. Hit wuz screamin' an hit's maw 'n paw wuz screamin' 'n jumpin' up 'n down.

I figgered they wudn't no better time to git out'uv thar. So, I backed up 'n I backed up 'til I wuz back in the front room 'uv the cave.

The rain had let up. I run all the way home, run down in the celler, grabbed me a keg 'uv black powder under each arm an sum fuse an run all the way back.

I found the hole in the top 'uv the cave. I set one keg 'uv powder in the hole an lit the fuse. When hit went off, hit blowed the whole top 'uv that mountain down, hole 'n all. Kivered everthang over.

I run down to the mouth'uv the cave whur I first went in an set the other keg inside an lit the fuse. Hit blowed the side 'uv the mountain down an closed the cave fer good.

I set down on a stump to rest. I'd done a good day's work 'n saved the country frum a turible disaster.

Suddenly, over head, I heerd wings flappin'. I looked up 'n thar wuz the male 'n female eagle. I'd blowed up the cave without makin' shore they wuz still in thar! I'd got the baby, but not the old ones.

The big female eagle swooped down with them sharp claws 'n grabbed me by my arms. Then, the male eagle grabbed my legs 'n they flew in different directions. They wuz pullin' me apart!

Ahhhh! Crack! I wuz fightin so hard the bed broke 'n I woke up. Ye'll never ketch me eatin' barbeque bar meat, green apple pie, 'n choklit cake at ten thirty at night agin. I betchy that!

Old Jonah's Bit 'uv Wisdom

If'n a bee stangs ye, an ye hain't got nothin' to put on hit, spit on sum mud an put hit on the stang. Hit'll draw out the pizen.

Old Jonah says . . .

Whilst yer gwine thru life, if'n hit gives ye a bad turn, don't jist set an lick yer wounds, git up an put sum salve on 'em.

———————

Don't make fun 'uv anybody less fortunate than you, 'cuz pay back's hard, brother. Pay back's hard.

———————

Ye kin only make so many trips to the well afore hit runs dry.

The Civil War brought pain, sufferin' 'n death to folks all over the country. Right hyar, in the Clinch Mountains, hit wudn't no different. Now, this hyar tale, to the best 'uv my recollectin', is true. My pappy has told hit to me fer as long as I kin remember, 'n my pappy didn't tell no lies that I knowed 'uv. Jist as ye start acrost Kent's Ridge, frum the Wardell end, they's three caves in the hillside. Story has hit, that one 'uv them goes all the way up to Claypool Hill 'n meets up with Big Chimbly Cave. When the road wuz widened 'n worked on a few yars ago, they jist about closed 'em off. But ye kin still see whur they wuz. They played a important role in this hyar little tale.

The Caves

"I jist don't see why ye have to git involved! If'n them Yankees find out yer helpin' the South, they'll burn us out 'n kill us all, jist like they have all them others they've ketched." the woman said as she poured black steamin' coffee into cups and set it on the table in front of the three men.

Then she poured some for herself, and continued to speak, "Ain't no use our gittin' kilt fer no more use than we air to the South."

One of the men spoke up, "Now, Sary, hit's true that we hain't able to do much fer the Confederacy. But, ever little bit helps, an if'n whut we do helps jist a little, then

111

hit's worth riskin' our lives. Now, that's the way all three 'uv us feel, so let's say no more 'bout hit." The three men finished their coffee, put on their hats and coats and stepped outside into the cold light of dawn.

As Sarah Davis put the men's empty cups into the dishwater, her thoughts went back to just two days before, when a stranger came by and in a low-voiced conversation, had given her husband this message: A wagon load of salt-peter, used in the making of gunpowder, was needed badly by the rebels over in Saltville.

By mixing sulfur, charcoal and saltpeter, you got black powder. The sulfur and charcoal, they had, but they needed saltpeter. The saltpeter mine in Saltville had played out and until they could find another source, they had to depend on hauling it from other places.

Sarah's husband, Roy and her two brothers, Jim and Blaine, dug all that day and the next in their saltpeter cave underneath the smokehouse. After loading the wagon al-most full, they finished filling it with ears of corn to hide the saltpeter. Then, they pulled it inside the barn to hide it from Northern sympathizers, who might be sneaking around.

Sarah's thoughts came back to the present. Today, Roy, Jim, and Blaine were to make the trip from Kent's Ridge to Saltville. A long trip which would require them to stay over and return the following day. Two days alone, she was not so much afraid for herself, but for Roy, Jim and Blaine. One could never tell when a Yankee patrol might be in the area. With the way the war was going, it might even be dangerous to the local citizens.

Two days for her to worry and fret, not knowing what was happening to her loved ones. She wanted to go with them, but someone had to stay here and take care of their small farm. Besides, Roy was firm that she not be dragged into the danger of their Confederate involvement.

She heard the wagon roll out of the barn lot and down the lane that led to the main road. She got some feed for the chickens and went to the henhouse to feed them and gather the eggs she had forgotten to gather yesterday. As she scattered feed for the chickens, she heard the baby cry from inside he house. She ran inside, picked up the child, and sat down in the rocking chair on the porch.

Sarah was humming a lullaby to the child and enjoying the cool morning breeze, when she heard the sound of many horses and the creaking of wheels. She stood up and walked down the steps to the gate, clutching the sleeping baby tightly in her arms.

The Yankee soldiers rode stiffly into the yard and came to a halt in front of the gate. Sarah quickly counted about thirty and they had with them two cannons.

The captain tipped his hat to Sarah and spoke in a clipped voice, "Morning, Mam. I would like to speak to your husband."

Sarah spoke quickly, "He ain't hyar. He went to take sum corn to have hit ground. Don't expect him back afore dark."

The captain spoke again. "To which mill did he take the corn?" he asked.

Sarah's mind raced quickly. She wanted to send them in the opposite direction of her husband and brothers. She

113

The captain tipped his hat to Sarah and spoke in a clipped voice . . .

114

remembered a mill, way down next to Abingdon, that her father went to once in a while. She stumbled over the words and hoped they wouldn't know she was lying, "They uh, he went to White uh, White's Mill 'bout forty miles frum hyar."

"Why did he go so far to grind his corn? There are mills closer that that." The captain sounded a little suspicious of her.

Sarah cleared her throat and spoke slowly, so as not to say the wrong thing. "My paw, he lives down that a way 'n he wuz gwine to pick up sum lumber that paw sawed fer us to build another room onto the house."

That seemed to satisfy the captain. He said, "Well, Mam, we'd like to water our horses at your trough if you don't mind. Then, we'll be on our way. Tell your husband that we're a scouting party for General Burbridge. He'll be along sometime tomorrow and if your husband or any of his friends are Southern sympathizers, or if they consider themselves rebels, they had better stay hidden. Because the general is not in any mood to be lenient nor is he taking prisoners. He's on a forced march to Wytheville to destroy the railroads and crush the blasted Confederates, there."

The soldiers watered their horses and then rode off. Sarah sank, trembling onto the porch steps. She wanted to see which way they went, but she was afraid they would see her and return and force her to tell the truth.

She put the baby back to bed and set about doing her chores, trying to keep her mind off her fears. When night came, she lit a lamp and fixed something to eat for herself and the baby. But, she pushed her's aside. She just couldn't git anything past the lump of fear in her throat.

115

She took the rifle down from over the fireplace and checked to see if it was loaded. She opened the door and called the dog upon the porch. Then, she closed the door and slid the bolt home.

Sarah sat for a while, mending her brother, Blaine's shirt by lamplight. Then, as her eyes became tired, she arose and took the baby from it's cradle and laid it in her bed. Tonight, he would be close to her, should anything happen.

Sarah didn't know how long she had been asleep, but the barking of the dog woke her with a start. She reached for the gun and without lighting the lamp, she made her way through the darkness to the window. She pulled aside the curtain, just a little, and she saw a shadow of men in the moonlight. She heard the creaking of wheels and then a large, dark shape loomed in front of the barn.

She gasped! Why, it was their wagon and that was her husband leading the horses and wagon quietly into the barn. In just a short time, she heard a low rapping on the door. She slid the bolt back and her husband slipped inside. Sarah started to light the lamp.

Roy spoke in a whisper, "Sary, don't! Don't light that lamp. Go on back to bed. Hit'll be daylight soon."

"But, Roy, whut's gwine on? Ye ain't had time to git the wagon to Saltville. Please tell me whut happened!"

Roy sank into a chair. Sarah could tell he was worn out. Bone tard, Roy allus said.

"Sary," he said, and he took her hand. "We almost run head on into a bunch 'uv 'em blasted Yankees. We jist barely got turned 'round 'n headed back on the old road.

116

Son of a gun, if'n we didn't run into another bunch, cumin' up behind us. 'Bout forty 'uv 'em 'n they had two cannons with 'em. We managed to hide the wagon in a big sink hole over in Burke's Garden. We had to go that fer out'uv our way to git away frum 'em. We've been dodgin' 'em 'n workin' our way back ever since.

We heerd sum'uv 'em talkin'. We wuz that close to 'em. They wuz talkin' 'bout a skirmish over at the Cedar Bluffs. Seems like they didn't wait fer General Burbridge to git hyar. Sum'uv 'em Yanks tangled with our boys 'n our boys fit 'em a while 'n jist disappeared into the woods."

Sarah throwed her arms around Roy's neck and sobbed, "Roy, them Yankees wuz by hyar early today, lookin' fer ye. They said Burbridge wud be hyar sumtime tomorrow an if anybody's sympathetic to the South, they had better stay out'uv sight."

She continued, "Now, with this skirmish, Burbridge will be mad as a hornet. An he'll take hit out on you 'n Jim 'n Blaine 'n anybody else that gits in his way."

She stopped and gripped Roy's arm tighter. "Whur's Jim 'n Blaine? Air they alright?"

Roy put his hands on her shoulder to calm her down. "Yes, Sary, thur alright. Blaine twisted his ankle purty bad, but, he'll be alright. They're out in the barn unhitchin' the team 'n keepin' a eye out fer truble."

Roy paced the room. "We got to find sumwhur to hide that saltpeter 'til 'em Yankees move on out'uv hyar. If'n they find hit, they'll know we air on the side 'uv the Confederacy. An, they'll shoot us down like dogs."

Roy was mumbling to himself, but Sarah could hear

him and the fear gripped her heart. She thought, how happy they had been a few short years ago, when she and Roy were married and had bought this farm. It was good, rich land. It grew almost anything they needed. Roy and her brothers had built this strong cabin and everything was going along wonderfully.

Then, two years ago, the baby was born. A son, so that Roy would have someone to love; to teach how to fish; and hunt; and later on, someone to help him on the farm. Sarah had made such wonderful plans for them all. And then, just a few months ago, war had broken out between the North and the South.

Roy, Jim and Blaine felt very strongly about the South's stand and had done what they could to help her. It kept them hiding and on edge all the time, now. Sarah's wonderful plans came crashing down around her ears.

"That's hit!" The sharpness of Roy's voice brought her thoughts back to the present. "That's hit, Sary! We'll unload hit in the caves! Nobody ever goes 'round 'em, an then, when the Yanks air gone, we'll load 'er up agin 'n take hit to Saltville. We'll do hit tonight, atter dark."

"I'll git Jim to drive the wagon over thar, now, afore hit gits daylight 'n hide hit in them thick laurel bushes, whur nobody kin see hit. Then, tomorrow night, we'll unload hit in the caves." He stepped out the door 'n closed it, leaving Sarah with a sinking feeling in the pit of her stomach.

All the next day, Sarah went about her work, praying for night to hurry and come, so they could get the saltpeter hidden. It seemed like everything she did went wrong. She burned the four loaves of bread she was baking. A bird

118

flew in the house, a sign of death, and to top everything else off, the baby stuck it's hand to the hot stove and burned a big blister on it. That made him fretful and whinny all day. By the time the sun went down, Sarah was a bundle of nerves and almost in tears.

As soon as supper was over, Roy and her brothers slipped out and headed for the caves. They pushed the wagon up against the mouth of the cave and began to unload the saltpeter. They put a canvas tarp on the ground, loaded it full, then carried it into the cave.

There were three caves, side by side. Two of them went for miles under ground. Some said that one went all the way to what is now Claypool Hill and came out in a large cavern, called Chimney Cave. The cave in which the three men were working was just one small room with the ceiling just barely high enough for them to stand. The only way into the cave was through the front.

They had almost finished unloading the wagon when a loud voice broke through the night. A sharp command, "You, in the cave! Come out with your hands over your heads! If you have any weapons, throw them out, first."

Roy, Jim and Blaine froze, their hearts in their throats. Slowly, without a sound, Roy reached for his rifle. Jim and Blaine eased up to the back of the wagon and got their rifles that were leaning against the wheels.

A shot rang out and ricocheted off the cave wall. Roy squatted beside Jim and Blaine and said, "Them's Yanks fer shore, boys! We're caught, shore as sartin!"

"But how did they know 'bout us bein' fer the South, in the first place?" Jim said. "I betchy hit's that low down polecat, Bill Jones! That varmint moved onto the ridge a yar ago 'n he never liked us. I figger he's a Yank sympathizer, spyin' on us. I've seed him pokin' 'round our place 'n your'n several times."

Another shot rang out. Then a voice. "This is your last chance, boys. We know you're working with the rebs. Come on out. You're our prisoners."

Jim poked his rifle over the wagon bed and fired. He heard someone yell and then curse. "I thank I hit one'uv 'em dirty dogs, Roy!"

Several shots whinned off the cave and the wagon. Blaine limped over and said, "We ain't got but two more shots. What air we gwine to do? We can't give up. They'll kill us, shore. Sary said yesterd'y, they wudn't takin' no prisoners. They'll shoot us 'er hang us."

They heard the voice again. "Forward, men! Shoot when you see them. Wound them if you can. I want to hang them and make an example to teach the other good citizens of this community a lesson."

Roy turned to his brothers-in-law, "Boys, thur cumin' in! Quick! Git me that keg 'uv sulfur over thar by the far wall. I'm gwine to build a sulfur far! Hit'll be so hot an the smoke'll be so thick, they kan't git in 'til hit dies down. Maybe hit'll give us time to bust through the wall into one'uv the other caves."

He pulled the rear of the wagon as far back into the mouth of the cave as he could and poured the sulfur all over it. He piled on leaves and brush that had blown into the cave, and lit it. The fire blazed up. The thick acrid smoke filled the air outside.

Jim and Blaine eased up to the back of the wagon and got their rifles.

The Yankees were shouting and cursing.

Jim grabbed a pick and so did Blaine. Roy took a sledge hammer. They all began pounding and digging at the wall, trying to break through to the next cave. They were fighting a brave, hard battle, but fate was not on their side.

Outside the wind had started blowing and instead of the smoke going outside, it caused it to blow back inside the cave. No matter how desperately hard they tried, the three men could not break through the wall. Rather than be shot or hung by the Yankees, they sank onto the cave floor and waited bravely for the suffocation they knew would come.

When the thick smoke cleared, the soldiers cautiously entered the cave. They found the three men huddled together, dead. Their idea had been a good one if it had not backfired. The captain gave the order and the dead men were thrown across the backs of horses and led away.

From the porch steps, Sarah could hear gunfire. She twisted her apron tighter and leaned against the porch post. Tears were rolling down her face.

For a while, all was quiet. Then, she heard horses hooves coming up the lane. The soldiers rode slowly into the yard. The sergeant dismounted, pushed the three dead men's bodies off the horses, into the dust of the yard. The captain arrogantly tipped his hat, gave a signal, and they all rode away from the farm at a gallop.

Sarah walked numbly down the steps. It was like she was in a daze. She knelt beside her husband, her finger tracing a line down his cheek. She kissed her brothers

gently, but no more tears came. They had all been cried out.

She pulled herself erect and walked to the barn. She found a shovel and dragging it behind her, she walked into the woods. Sarah spent all morning digging three graves. The rest of the day, she spent wrapping her loved ones in sheets and dragging them to the graves.

When the shadows of late evening fell over the valley, Sarah entered the house and sat down at the table. Her eyes were a blank, glassy stare. The baby began to cry, but Sarah did not hear. She just sat and stared and stared.

This story was told to me by my dad, Carson Vencill, as a true story. It supposedly, did happen. However, I have taken some liberties and added some angles in order to make it more interesting. The men did die by sulfur smoke inhalation, fighting for the South. They did die in one of the caves on Kent's Ridge road, on the Wardell end.

Old Jonah's Mush

Back when I wuz a young'un, vittles wuz a little skeerce sumtimes. But, my maw had a way 'uv fixin' good thangs out'n almost nuthin'. Take fer instance, mush. Jist put sum water in a pot, pour in a cup'uv corn meal 'n cook. If'n ye got milk 'n sugar, pour hit over the mush 'n eat. If'n ye haint got milk 'n sugar, jist eat hit like hit is. But, now, hyar cums the tasty way, I thank.

Fried Mush

Put two cups 'uv water in a pot 'n boil. Add one cup'uv corn meal, salt 'n pepper. Cook mush 'til hit gits to whur hit's good 'n thick. Pour hit in a bowl 'n let hit stand over night. (Hit'll thicken more.) Next morning, git out'uv bed, put sum smoked bacon grease in a skillet 'n heat hit real hot. Cut the mush in cakes 'n place in the hot grease. Fry hit 'til brown. Sum'uv the best food ye'll ever eat. An that's the gospel truth!

The Old Timers hyar in the Clinch Mountains knowed the importance 'uv stickin' together, thru thick 'n thin. Hit shore made ye feel good to have good neighbors. Hit still does.

Good 'n Urly

One time they wuz two fellers whut lived crost the ridge frum me. Thur farms jined each other. One 'uv the feller's name wuz Ben Good 'n the other wuz named Urly Byrd.

Ever since they wuz young 'n cum into the valley, they had worked side by side, never hesitatin' to lend each other a hand when hit wuz needed. They helped each other build thur cabins, plant thur crops, fight off wolves, panthers 'n injuns. They got along like two fleas on a hound dog's tail. Now, that's gittin' along real fine, I'm hyar to tell ye!

But, ye know, thur wives wuz plum different. They never did like each other. Cudn't stand the ground the other'n stood on. An, they never made no bones 'bout hit. They never got together lessen they got in a fight.

Sumtimes, word fights. Sumtimes, knock-down, drag-out fights. If'n ye wuz passin' by thur farms on worsh day,

One wud hang up a piece 'uv laundry 'n let fly
with 'em yar-blisterin' words.

ye shore wud want to put yer hands over yer yars 'n run on by, 'cuz yer shore to git 'em blistered by the hot 'n harsh words. One wud hang up a piece 'uv laundry 'n let fly with 'em yar-blisterin' words. Then the other'n wud hang up a piece 'uv clothes 'n let fly a strang 'uv scorchers.

Now, this had been gwine on fer many yars 'n all four 'uv 'em wuz gittin' on in age. So, Ben 'n Urly set out to try 'n settle thangs betwixt thur wives. They set 'em down 'n talked 'n pleaded 'til they wuz blue in the face 'n so tard they went to bed two hours sooner than they allus did. Yessir, they went to bed at five o'clock in the evenin'.

They tuk thur wives into town to one'uv 'em fancy hotels 'n eatin' places. I thank they call 'em restrunts.

Ben 'n Urly figgered if'n they let 'em eat together in town 'n shop together, they might see that they cud git along. But, Ben's wife, Effie, complained that her steak wuz tuffer'n a sow's yar. Urly's wife, Corine, said her meatloaf looked a whole lot like Effie's face.

That little remark brought a quick response frum Effie in the form 'uv a bowl 'uv chicken gravy over Corine's head. That little incident brought an end to supper.

The next day, the two men dug into thur pockets fer sum'uv thur hard-earned money 'n sent the two wimmen off together, shoppin'.

They managed to git into the dress shop together 'n as wimmen will do, they fergot thur hate fer each other, as they oohed 'n ahhed over the purty dresses, hats 'n shoes. But, the truce, hit didn't last long.

Effie told Corine she looked like old man Jenkin's mule in the hat she wuz tryin' on. When Effie tried on a pair

127

'uv shoes, 'n they didn't fit, Corine said she didn't thank they wuz anywhur in town whur they sold shoes, that fit cows. They left the shop in a huff!

'Bout half way back to the hotel, Corine 'n Effie got into a fight over who had the purtiest dress. They kicked off thur shoes 'n wuz rollin' in the street, pullin' hair, kickin' 'n bitin' fer all that wuz in 'em.

They wuz gwine at hit so hot 'n heavy, they didn't see the stagecoach flyin' 'round the corner 'n hit cudn't stop! They wuz fussin' 'n carryin' on when they tuk off fer Heaven 'n Saint Peter said they wudn't no way he wuz gwine to let 'em in Heaven to carry on like that. Why, he said, they'd never be no more peace up thar! So, he sent 'em down to see the 'ol devil.

The 'ol devil heerd 'em fussin' 'n fightin' 'n he sent two 'uv his young'uns out to show 'em inside. The wimmen kept on fussin'. They stopped long 'enuf to stomp 'em two little devils 'n kicked 'em back into the far.

The devil hollered up to Saint Peter 'n said, "Peter, git down hyar! We got to work sumthin' out hyar. They hain't no way I'm lettin' 'em two come in hyar."

Saint Peter said, "Well, they shore hain't gittin' up hyar in heaven."

So, Saint Peter 'n the devil, they made a little spot, oh, 'bout ten acres, right betwixt heaven 'n hell 'n put 'em thar. That seemed to work fer both 'uv 'em.

Wal, now, Ben 'n Urly buried thur wives thar in town 'n went on home. They unhitched thur horses 'n set down on the porch 'n talked 'bout how hit wuz best they left thur wives buried in town. 'Cuz, fer the first time in

They wuz gwine at hit so hot 'n heavy, they didn't see the stage-coach flyin' 'round the corner 'n hit cudn't stop!

129

thur married lives, they had peace.

They hired a fiddler 'n a banjer player 'n opened a barrel 'uv hard cider 'n they danced 'n party'd; jist the two 'uv 'em fer three days 'n nights. Then, they set on thur porches 'n rested 'til they got tard 'uv restin'. The two men wur the happiest they'd been in yars. They worked together 'n had a wonderful time.

Time passed 'n then one day, when Urly wuz ninety-two, he went out to the outhouse 'n didn't cum back. Ben went to look fer him 'n fell over a stick 'n hit his head on the trunk 'uv a apple tree.

When the neighbors found the men, they tuk 'em to thur homes, had a wake, 'n then, they buried 'em on the little hill, overlookin' thur farms. Like they allus wanted to be.

Atter a couple 'uv months, the worms got in old Urly's coffin 'n soon they wudn't nuthin' left 'uv him but bones.

Then. one day, they dug up Corine 'n Effie an replanted 'em beside Ben 'n Urly. Them graves got to rockin' 'n ye cud hyar them wimmen fussin' 'n carryin' on.

Old Ben, he kicked the top off'n his coffin. He kicked the dirt off'n his grave 'n hitched up his new buryin' bib overhauls 'n went home. He kicked his chur back agin the wall 'n dozed off. Wudn't no way, he wuz gwine to wait 'til Judgement Day, laying thar listnin' to them dang fool wimmen, a-rantin' 'n a-ravin'!

Pore 'ol Urly! Too bad, he wuz so dad blasted tight! If'n he'd spent more on his coffin, hit wudn't a-leaked, him 'n Ben cud've laid thar 'n jawed 'n jist had a good time.

Wal, I guess the best way to end this hyar story an this hyar book, is to simply say that the Urly Byrd allus gits the worm. But, by crackys, ye jist kan't keep a Good man down.

See ye next book. Heh, heh, heh.

GLOSSARY

A
acrost - across
afore - before
agin - against
air - are
allus-always
anythang - anything
atter - after

B
backards - backwards
banjer - banjo
bar - bear
betchy - bet you
betwixt - between
bile - boil
blue -sad
booger -monster
brang - bring
breakfust - breakfast
bresh - brush
britches - breeches, pants

C
chimbly - chimney
choklit - chocolate
chur - chair
clomb - climb
clost - close
crost - crossed
cud - could
cudn't - could not
cum - come
cuz - because

D
docktered - doctored

drank - drink
drapped - dropped

E
'em - them
'enuf - enough
'er - or
'et - ate
everthang - everything

F
far - fire
feller - fellow
fer - for
ferever - forever
figger - figure
figgered - figured
ford - forehead
fount - found
frum - from

G
git - get
goin' - going
gwine - going

H
haint - isn't, ghost
heerd - heard
hesh - hush
hit - it
hit'd - it had
hit'll - it will
holler - hollow
hongry - hungry
hunnert - hundred
hurrycane - hurricane

133

hyar - here

I
idee - idea
if'n -if
injuns - indians
I'se - I was

J
jined - joined
jist - just

K
kant - can't
keer - care
keerful - careful
kilt - killed
kin - can
kiver - cover
kivers - quilts, bedding, (such as
    Put more kivers on the bed.)

L
laigs - legs
larn't - learned
leven - eleven
lopyared - lopeared
'lowed- allowed

M
mater - tomato
maw - mother
mebbe - may be
mite - might,little, (as in, Hit's a
    mite early.)

N
'n - and
narrer - narrow
narrered - narrowed
nary - not

ner - nor
nigh - near, close
noggin' - head
nowhur - no where
nuthin' - nothing

O
off'n - off of
onliest - only
onyun - onion
ort - ought

P
pap - father
paragoric - medicine
paw - father
pitcher - picture
pizen - poison
plum - plumb
purty - pretty
purtiest - prettiest

R
rang - ring
rared - reared, leaned
retch - reached
ridiklas - ridiculous
rurn't - ruined

S
Saterd'y - Saturday
sartin - certain
seed - saw
shadders - shadows
shet - shut
shinnied - climbed
shore - sure
shorely - surely
shuk - shook

sich - such
sityeated - situated
skeerd -scared
skint - skinned
sot - set
spoilt - spoiled
strang - string
suddin - sudden
sum - some
sumthin' - something
sumtimes - some times
swallered - swallowed

T

tain't - isn't
tard - tired
teched - touched
terbacker - tobacco
terbacky - tobacco
turific - terrific
thang - thing
thank - think
thar - there
that'ud - that would
thru - through
thunk - thought
thur - their
'til - until
tommyhawk - tomahawk
tother - the other
truble - trouble
tuk - took
turible -terrible
twarn't - wasn't

U

uster - used to
'uv - of

V

vagrus - vicious, mean
victry - victory
vittles - food

W

wal - well
whilst - while
whur - where
whut - what
whuther - whether
worsh - wash
writ - written
wropped - wrapped
wud - would
wudn't - wouldn't
wur - were
wuz - was

Y

yaller - yellow
yander - yonder
yars - ears, years
ye - you
yep - yes
yer - your
yerself - yourself
yit - yet
young'uns - young ones, children
you'uns - you all

Learn more about Jerry Vencill as "Old Jonah, the Storyteller" by contacting him at JO-NAH Productions, P.O. Box 412, Pounding Mill, VA 24637. Or contact him by telephone at (540) 964-2027.

If you or your organization is interested in having him perform at a function, he will be happy to give you pertinent information concerning price and scheduling, either by letter or over the phone.

He performs several acts including:
        Old Jonah, the Storyteller
        Amos Skillet, Circuit-riding Preacher
        The Grave Digger
        Historical and Biblical Dramas

The following items are also available:
        Old Jonah's Book of Tales (the first Book of
        Tales of a series, published in 1997) $14.95

        Old Jonah and the Bee Tree (a 32-page story-
        coloring book for the youngsters) $5.95

        Tall Tales of Long Ago (a one-hour Video
        with Old Jonah telling stories in a mountain
        setting) A must for Old Jonah fans. $19.95

        Old Jonah Pouting Doll (A realistic doll, depicting
        Old Jonah in his Mountainman costume) $30.00

Please add $4.00 shipping and handling for each book and video. Add $6.00 shipping and handling for each doll. Send money order to JO-NAH Productions, P.O. Box 412, Pounding Mill, VA 24637